ALL'S FAE IN LOVE AND WAR

THE PARANORMAL PI FILES - BOOK SIX

JENNA WOLFHART

This book was produced in the UK using British English, and the setting is London. Some spelling and word usage may differ from US English.

All's Fae in Love and War

Book Six in The Paranormal PI Files

Cover Design by Covers by Juan

Copyright © 2019 by Jenna Wolfhart

All rights reserved.

No part of this book may be reproduced in any form or by any electronic or mechanical means, including information storage and retrieval systems, without written permission from the author, except for the use of brief quotations in a book review.

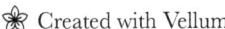

ALSO BY JENNA WOLFHART

The Supernatural Spy Files
Confessions of a Dangerous Fae

The Paranormal PI Files
Live Fae or Die Trying
Dead Fae Walking
Bad Fae Rising
One Fae in the Grave
Innocent Until Proven Fae
All's Fae in Love and War

The Bone Coven Chronicles
Witch's Curse
Witch's Storm
Witch's Blade
Witch's Fury

Protectors of Magic
Wings of Stone
Carved in Stone

Bound by Stone
Shadows of Stone

Otherworld Academy
A Dance with Darkness
A Song of Shadows
A Touch of Starlight

Dark Fae Academy
A Cage of Moonlight
A Heart of Midnight

Order of the Fallen
Ruinous
Nebulous

1

The full moon illuminated the streets of London, but it did little to drown the darkness. I hunkered in the shadows of a weeping angel and watched as two gravediggers struck the dirt with their shovels. It was too dark to see their faces. One's form was large, thick, and commanding while the other's was thin like the crackling bare branches of the nearby tree.

My thighs groaned from how long I'd spent squatting in the darkness. We'd gotten an anonymous tip that the Fianna would be here this night, and I'd been unable to resist the temptation to check things out, despite the likelihood that this was nothing more than a trap.

Of course, Aed and his fellow Fianna were an hour deep into digging this grave. If it were a trap, it was a pretty committed one.

I shifted on my feet and turned toward Balor. He was the mirror image of me, his powerful form obscured by the twin weeping angel to mine. His single orange eye gleamed in the darkness. Despite the creepy atmosphere and the danger right at our fingertips, my heart flipped once, twice, thrice.

Things had been...strained between us in the weeks since we'd taken back the Court. A huge part of that could be blamed on the revelations we'd had about each other. Both of us were the reincarnated forms of ancient faeries, sometimes enemies, sometimes lovers, but always inexplicably twined. The magic was pushing us together and pulling us apart, testing us to see which way the coin would land.

On love. Or on hate.

But I also knew, deep down inside, no matter how much Balor bowed his head to me, part of the tension between us was because I now sat on his throne.

It scared me, knowing how much Balor valued his rule over the Crimson Court. He had devoted his entire life to serving his fae. They were his subjects, but he'd always considered them so much more. He had done everything in his power to protect them, he had sacrificed so much. The love he felt for them far surpassed his love for anything else.

Deep down inside, I knew that if we landed on enemies, it would be because of this.

He gave a slow nod and inched slowly out of the shadows to show me that his sword was ready for battle. With a deep breath, I nodded back, my heartbeat racing. It was just the two of us tonight. With the current state of the Court, we couldn't bring the whole team with us. Kyle, Moira, and Elise were keeping watch over the fae, on high alert for any sign of Nemain. They couldn't even risk walking outside those gleaming double doors for fear she'd be lying in wait to whisper her orders into their pointed ears.

We might be inside the building, but Nemain had gotten into their heads. All she had to do was speak the words out loud, and the fae of the Crimson Court would do whatever she wanted to command.

But not for long.

I tightened my grip on my sword and scuttled through the quiet graveyard. I'd been practicing my stealth. But while I'd gotten better, I wasn't good enough. Aed heard me before I got halfway across the lawn.

Slowly, he turned, his deep-set orange eyes glowing in the thick darkness that permeated the London night. His lips twisted up into a wicked grin as he stepped away from the makeshift grave and spun the shovel in his beefy hands.

"Well, look who it is," he called in a lilting Irish accent. Aed and the rest of the Fianna, the band of fae warriors, were from House Futrail, an ancient stone house that sat in the midst of the rolling Irish hills. Nemain had brought them here, to London. They were the best warriors in the world.

I came to a slow stop and sized up his companion. He was a fae I'd never seen before. Tall, built extraordinarily like a waif, with daggers for ears poking through purple hair. He looked nothing like any Fianna I'd ever met—most were pounds upon pounds of pure muscle, bodies sculpted like gods.

"Yep, it's me again. Did you really think you could avoid me forever?"

Balor stayed behind in the shadows, watching and waiting. We didn't want Aed and his mate to know he was here until absolutely necessary. Let them think they had the upper hand.

Aed's grin widened. "Nope. Quite the opposite. We've been sending out bat signals the past few days, hoping you'd finally pick up on one. And here you are."

My heart thumped, and I wet my lips. I fought the urge to glance behind me to where I knew Balor was lurking in the shadows. So, they'd been ready and waiting. We'd expected as much. No need to panic.

Yet.

Rolling back my shoulders, I took a step closer to Aed. His friend stood with his feet frozen to the churned-up ground, so silent he could have been a ghost. "And here I am." I flicked my gaze around the graveyard, frowning. "Let me guess. You thought you'd dig a hole to bury my body."

Aed chuckled. "No, but that would have been a damn good idea, wouldn't it, Midir?"

The purple-haired waif gave a slight nod.

"What we're doing here tonight is none of your concern," Aed continued. "I didn't lure you out of hiding to kill you."

"I haven't been in hiding. I've been sitting on the damn throne."

"I'll give you that." He twirled the shovel in his hands one more time and then stabbed it into the ground, where he leaned against the wooden pole. "Look, you and I, we've never gotten along."

I snorted. "To put it mildly."

From day one, Aed and I had been at odds, even before Nemain had come into the picture. He'd stood beside Fionn when he'd twisted his sneaky little nose into the Crimson Court, in an attempt to steal the crown away from Balor. We'd fought, time and time again. Neither of us ever won, but we never lost either.

"That said, I have some respect for who and what you are," he continued with an arched, meaningful brow that waggled like a caterpillar.

Ah, so now I saw where this was going. When Nemain had escaped the dungeons, she'd filled Aed in on what she'd learned. That I was the current reincarnation of the Morrigan, which meant I was supposed to be the most powerful fae alive. I'd had doubts about the whole reincarnation thing—it had been hard as hell to wrap my mind around it, particularly because I was only half-fae. But I'd managed to come around to the idea I had several past lives. But being the most powerful fae ever? That wasn't me. No way in hell.

At least not yet.

"You have respect for the Morrigan. Not me," I said quietly. In the past, Aed had made it more than clear just how much he wished he could see my head on a pike.

He shrugged. "That may have been true for a time, but you are the Morrigan, Clark, whether I like it or not. That changes things, especially how the fae of the world see you."

Tightening the grip on my sword, I frowned. "Just get on with it. Why did you want me to come here tonight?"

"Nemain has a proposition for you."

My heart thumped. "Nemain. Of course she does."

"Don't act so surprised. Surely you saw this coming."

I had, in fact, not.

"If Nemain has 'a proposition' for me, then why didn't she come to me herself?" I let out a strained laugh. "It's not like she's ever been shy before now."

"Nemain has other things she must attend to at the moment. Besides, she knew you'd likely charge in with steel before listening to a word she had to say."

She wasn't wrong about that. But that wasn't what had caught my full attention. Nemain was attending to something else, but what? My entire point in coming here tonight was to get information about her plans, and yet I'd been sidetracked by Aed's surreal attempt at conversation. Before he could change the subject—and the course of his thoughts—I dove straight into his mind.

...busy trying to woo the Ivory Court to her side. Just need to make sure Clark doesn't find out Nemain is at House Futrail, even if she does agree to join our side...

Quickly, I pulled out of his head before he could figure out what I'd done. I'd gotten better at hiding my mind-reading abilities, but I still couldn't obscure my trick completely. If he asked me a question out loud while I was diving through the rivers of his thoughts, he'd get nothing but a blank expression for an answer.

"Okay, I'll give you that," I finally said. "You're a better negotiator than she is, though not by much. Don't think I've forgotten how many times you've tried to chop off my head."

"Maybe we can make it up to each other." His voice dropped low as he crossed the space between us, coming to a stop a mere inch away. I swallowed hard and kept my gaze forward, knowing that my mating bond with Balor would cause him to go wild with jealousy at seeing another male so close to my body. Now was not the time for him to go wild with rage. I was two seconds away from hearing whatever it was Aed wanted to say to me, and we needed to know what it was.

"Explain," I said quietly.

"You're the Morrigan. Your powers are...impressive. In your past lives, you've been Queen of the Fae many times, but you don't seem like the kind of girl to crave power. Maybe the Morrigan does, but Clark Cavanaugh doesn't. Am I right?"

A strange lump formed in my stomach, one that made me feel a little sick. I did not like the direction this was heading.

"I have no desire to speak power with you."

A strange smile curled on his lips. "Nemain has been alive for a very long time. She has seen much and learned even more. She should be the Queen of Faerie. If you help her in the fight, she will give you the Crimson Court throne."

I blinked. It was all I could manage to do beneath the weight of his words. My skin twitched as I thought about Balor in the shadows just behind us. I didn't need to see him to imagine how he looked. Face transformed by rage, body tense with a trembling power that begged for relief.

"That makes no sense," was all I could manage to say. "If Nemain wants to be Queen, why would she encourage someone else to sit on a throne?"

"You wouldn't be on the throne as a Queen or

Princess yourself. You'd merely be the...steward. She would still have ultimate rule."

"Right. Well, you can tell her she can shove her proposition right up her ass. You were right about one thing. I don't want power. I have no desire for it. But that doesn't mean I'm going to let Nemain take it. After everything she's done, I would never help her become Queen of Faerie."

Aed chuckled and gave a slow nod. "Yeah, that's what I thought you'd say."

I stiffened, fingers tightening around the hilt of my sword. Until now, he'd been somewhat pleasant in the hope that he could get something from me. Now that he knew there was no chance in hell I was joining their side, he would no doubt charge, just as he always did.

But he merely shook his head and turned back toward his grave, motioning for his purple-haired buddy to join him. "Nemain ordered me not to fight you. She wants you for herself. 'Course, that means you could stab me in the back if you want, while I stand here, digging this grave for a fallen friend."

Irritation bubbled up inside of me, and I growled. I twisted on my heels and stomped away, angrily shoving my sword back into its sheath. I hated that Nemain knew me as well as she did. I hated that she had the ability to play me. She knew I'd never stab Aed in the back while he was burying his dead. And she knew I'd never join her.

She was playing a game, and I didn't know the rules.

2

Balor reacted much as I expected. Back in the bowels of the command station, he attacked the punching bag with the kind of intensity that would make a normal person scream and run in the opposite direction. But I stood and watched, leaning against the concrete wall, quietly waiting for his anger to turn my way.

Sweat gleaming on his brow, his punches finally slowed to half-hearted jabs. He turned to me, ripped his shirt over his head to reveal a six-pack glistening beneath the glowing lights. I swallowed hard and fought the urge to jump on top of him. Ever since we'd bonded, my need for him had been insatiable. I wanted him pretty much every moment of every day.

He growled and stalked toward me. Magic sparked in the air, a dark cloud of power spun between us, from the very depths of Faerie itself. He narrowed his eyes as it thickened between us, and all the fight and rage went out of him like a lightbulb punched in the middle of the night.

"I can't stand this," he said, stalking over to the wall to drag his fingers across the myriad of blades the guards had collected over the years.

"Can't stand Nemain's plan, or...?"

He whirled toward me, eye alight with danger. "I can't stand this magic. We wasted so much time, you and me, dancing around our desires until we cemented our bond. Now, you're out of arm's reach from me yet again. It's driving me mad."

I sucked in a deep breath, trying to ignore the frantic beat of my heart. Truth be told, I felt the same. Every time Balor and I came even close to touching, the magic would swirl, lighting would charge through the air, and we'd be forced to stand apart. We'd already hurt one person with our combined magic. We couldn't risk giving into our desires and hurting more.

"We'll figure it out," I said quietly, though I barely believed the words. It seemed impossible.

"Meanwhile, Nemain is taking over the world, by using my own damn throne as bait."

I didn't want to correct him. It was my throne now.

"It shows she's not as smart as she thinks," I said. "I was never going to take that bait."

He scowled. "No doubt she's holding it up for others as well. You said Aed was thinking about the Ivory Court?"

I gave a nod, relieved that we were onto an easier topic than the magic-soaked desire swirling between our bodies. Strategies, mission ideas, enemy moves. That was easy footing. We'd been there before, many times. And there was no threat of this kind of talk escalating into something more.

"She still plans to get them to join her side, but it sounds like she hasn't left yet. She's up to something at House Futrail, something she doesn't want me to know about." I frowned. "It doesn't make much sense."

Balor grabbed a short curved blade from the wall and spun it through deft fingers. "Nemain's moves often don't make sense until they do. We'll look back on this and understand in the worst way possible."

I crossed my arms over my chest and scanned his unreadable face. "You sound as though we're already defeated."

He let out a bitter laugh. "Aren't we? Our Court isn't even ours. No doubt she sees no rush in moving against us because she doesn't need to do a damn thing. The magic will ensure they will always defer to her."

"She's being cocky, thinking she can leave London while we're in her Court," I argued. "That will be her downfall. While she's looking elsewhere, we'll be preparing for this war."

He let out a sigh, tossed the blade to the sparring mat, and ran a hand down his tired face. "Faerie has not had war for so long. We have become accustomed to luxurious peace. Our warriors are few. Our hearts have grown soft. The fae of the Crimson Court will not survive a war."

His words shook through me, and I knew them to be true. In my visions of the past, there had been scores upon scores of warrior fae. Armies that covered fields. Now, each House had merely a few. And, even then, they were rarely needed. Some of the warrior fae from back then still lived on even now, but their training would be forgotten.

I sucked in a deep breath. What I was about to say next would not go over very well with Balor. He would tell me no, refuse to allow my next steps. But I was the leader of this Court now, not him.

"I want to go north and pay House Futrail a visit. If I can catch Nemain by surprise there, maybe I can finish this fight before we have to go to war."

Balor narrowed his eye and scowled. "That is a terrible idea."

"Is it?" I arched a brow. "She won't expect me."

"She will have Fianna surrounding her, even if she feels safe there."

"I'll take backup. Only those I trust."

Balor's scowl deepened. "It sounds like you not only want to go on a suicide mission but you want to go on it without me."

My heart lurched. This was it. The part I knew he'd struggle with the most. Truth be told, so would I. "You need to stay here and keep an eye on the Court. You're the only one who—"

"Elise," he said in a low growl.

"Is an amazing second," I said with a nod. "But you have been their Prince for years. They might no longer be bonded to you, but they love and respect you. They will feel better if you're here."

"Is that it?" He stalked toward me, and magic sparked in the air. "That is the only reason you wish to fight Nemain without me by your side?"

"You know that's not the only reason," I whispered, tears blurring my vision. "Whatever is happening between us is dangerous. It's volatile, and we can't seem to control it. If we go up north together, and our magic goes wild..."

"We could use it against Nemain," he argued.

"Or we could end up killing the whole damn House."

~

In the end, Balor begrudgingly agreed that we would be better off splitting our efforts. On one condition, of course. Backup had to be in the form of two beefy warriors with plenty of experience in the field. Time to pay a visit to my two exes.

After Tiarnan and Ronan had been imprisoned by Nemain, they'd formed a bond. So much so that Tiarnan had moved straight into Ronan's warehouse instead of joining us at the Court. He'd since then moved into the House, in order to help out with guard duty, but he still hung out with Ronan several times a week, crashing at the warehouse when he'd had too much to drink. I had to admit I found it more than a little strange. As far as I could tell, those two had only one thing in common. And that was me.

I strode through the shadowy streets after dodging the swarm of protestors that still camped outside of the Court, flicking my eyes left and right as I moved out of range of the blinding streetlights. Nemain might not be in town, but angry humans certainly were. The Mayor had ordered for supes to stay off the streets, particularly after dark. If we were caught out after curfew, they'd throw us behind bars. More than one fight had broken out because of the new rules.

Human cops sported broken noses, gashed shins, or worse, after a scuffle.

Not every London supe was willing to bow down before the rule of humans.

When I reached Ronan's old warehouse hidden within the depths of South London, I rapped my knuckles against the steel door. A moment later, a rattling sound filled the air as the door wheeled up before me. Ronan, with his scruffy beard and deep-set black eyes, peered out at me.

"Clark," he said in a gruff voice. "Didn't expect you to come calling here in the middle of the bloody night. Has something happened?"

"Yes and no," I said. "But more on the no side of things, to be honest."

He swore beneath his breath, but he motioned me inside. I ducked beneath the door and winced as it slammed shut behind me. As always, Ronan's warehouse residence was steeped in shadows. There was one small lamp lit in the far corner next to a TV and a ratty old couch. A cage hunkered in the opposite corner, all steel bars and blood stains.

Ronan liked to lock himself up when he couldn't fight his beastly rage. A fact I'd found unnerving when I'd first met him, but endearing now.

He crossed his arms over his chest and leaned against a column erected in the center of the room. "So, go on. Why are you here?"

"Where's Tiarnan? I thought he was hanging out here tonight," I said by way of an answer. "He needs to hear this, too."

Ronan grunted, shook his head, and disappeared through a door at the back. A moment later, he appeared with a very sleep-addled Tiarnan. His dark locks were bunched up, tiredness clouded his eyes. He didn't seem to have any idea what year it was, let alone why he'd been yanked out of bed. How many drinks did it take to get a fae drunk? *A lot*.

"The gang's all here," Ronan said. "Now, tell me what the hell is going on here, Clark."

"Nemain is in Ireland." I turned to Tiarnan. "At House Futrail. I want to go head her off there before she has a chance to make it to any other Court."

Tiarnan's beer-addled eyes widened with realisation. "You're going to try to kill her."

I winced. "I wouldn't put it quite like that. But yes. We have a very small window of opportunity here. She'll head to the Ivory Court any day now and try to convince them to join her side. If we get to her before she gets to the other Courts..."

"Huh." Ronan dragged his eyes to the warehouse door. "Where's your mate? Don't try to pretend he'd just let you go off on an insane murder mission without his broody presence."

"Balor is staying behind. It's…a long and complicated story that I don't think any of us want me to go into right now. But that's why I'm here. I can't go alone. I need both of you to come with me."

3

We were in the car within half an hour. It didn't take much to convince them to tag along, especially after Tiarnan had several espresso shots to sober him up. Ronan might have fled from London once to avoid the fight, but he was more than ready to make up for it now. Half a day of winding roads and a crisp ferry journey later, the three of us landed on the Irish shores that House Futrail called home.

It had only been a few months since I first laid eyes on House Futrail, but so much had happened since then, it felt like years. Ronan, Tiarnan, and I crouched behind a hill, the foreboding house rising up from the mossy ground like danger lurking in the shadows.

Tiarnan let out a low whistle and ducked beneath the crest of the hill. He shook his head, winced. "I never thought I'd be looking at my own house as a stranger. Damn Fionn."

"Damn Nemain," I muttered. "She's the reason you're not welcome there."

"All of this might be her fault, in the end, but violence was always brewing inside of Fionn. He would have gotten where he did all on his own, eventually."

"Maybe you're right," I said, remembering the crazed look in Fionn's eyes when he'd tried to sentence me to death.

"So, what's the plan, boss?" Ronan asked. He looked so out of place, doing his level best to hide his hulking mass in the tall blades of grass. A stealthy ninja he was not.

"Scope things out," I said with a nod. "See who comes and who goes. Since Nemain took over House Futrail, we've had next to no contact with them, other than Aed showing up now and again, lobbing threats and swords our way. We have no idea who is still here, what kind of army she's built, what they're doing."

"Surveillance." A sly grin spread across Tiarnan's face. "Your favourite."

"Don't start." I narrowed my eyes in his direction. "Annoy me enough, and I'll leave you to surveil all on your own."

His grin widened. "Empty threats. No way in hell you're not going to be here for the moment Nemain steps out of that house, if only so you can lob eye daggers *her* way."

"You overestimate my desire for eye dagger revenge." I turned toward him, raised my brow, and couldn't help but grin back. It had taken a lot for me to forgive what he'd done. Betrayal wasn't something that someone like me could forget lightly. But somehow, we'd gotten back to where we'd once been. I was glad we'd managed to work things out. Of course, I wasn't about to tell him that.

So, the three of us settled in on our little hill, keeping our eyes and ears open for anything that could give us an indication of what Nemain and the Fianna had planned.

Much to my annoyance, not a damn thing happened. For hours.

"Right." My elbows dug into the damp earth as I crawled closer to the crest of the hill. "We could spend the next week squatting here or I could get us in there in about five minutes."

Ronan arched a brow. "I'm not sure I like where this is going. You've got that look in your eye again. The one that means you're going to get us all into a shed load of trouble."

"I'm going to shift, get inside the building, and then let you inside," I said, ignoring his skeptical expression. "You know, like we did when we got inside the Crimson Court a few weeks back."

"And we all know how well that turned out," Tiarnan muttered beneath his breath.

In the end, it had worked out splendidly. We'd gotten the throne back from Nemain, and she'd buggered off into the shadows. Of course, in the short term, Tiarnan and Ronan had been forced to play the part of prisoner.

I grinned. "Don't worry. I'll protect you."

Ronan snorted. Tiarnan rolled his eyes. "I don't suppose there's any way we can talk you out of this?"

"You can try." I pushed up from the ground. "But you know it'll never work."

Quickly, I stole across the mossy ground and

kicked my feet into the air as my body transformed from fae into bird. Even though I had mastered the shift many weeks ago, I'd still continued my practice, aided by Ronan's grumpy words and a hell of a lot of motivation on my part. It was one of the few advantages I had over Nemain. She saw my shifter nature as a weakness. I saw it as a strength.

The ground disappeared beneath me as I soared through the air. Within moments, I found a cracked window and slipped inside the House, unbeknownst to the warrior inside, frowning at himself in the mirror. He flexed his bicep and frowned deeper. Even ancient fae weren't immune to body image issues.

Thankfully, his door was open, and I soared right on out of there before he could hear the flap of my wings. Down the corridor I went, passing door after door of housing for the fae who called this mansion their home. For a moment, I felt the constriction of my heart. These fae were against me, thanks to Nemain, but they were still part of the Crimson Court.

As part of the seven Courts around the world, the Crimson Court ruled over many Houses, mostly closely linked regionally. Those Houses were home to the fae who lived in the area. It was where they felt safe, where they were taken care of by the Master of the House.

There no longer was a Master of House Futrail. Not anymore. Not after Balor had killed Fionn, because of me.

And now I was on their doorstep, ready to fight.

I was the one responsible for their safety. And yet I was sneaking in here like an enemy of the night.

Spinning through the corridors, I vowed to make things right. Once we had regained control of the Court, I would select a powerful, trustworthy, honourable fae to act as Master of this House. And I would pledge to keep every fae here safe, even the Fianna who had fought so strongly against me.

It would be my duty as their Queen.

Finally, I reached the side door that Ronan and Tiarnan were watching for my signal. I shifted back into my fae form, hoping no one would stumble upon me and my nakedness. One downside of the whole shifter thing. We couldn't exactly take clothes with us.

I cracked open the door, poked out my head, and motioned frantically at the distant hillside where I knew they were waiting. Then, I shifted back into my bird and waited in the rafters for them to join me.

I fought better as a fae, but in bird form, I could scout ahead. People rarely looked up when hunting for enemies.

Footsteps thudded on the floor as the males slid through the door. Tiarnan barely made a sound, but Ronan the wolf was the furthest thing from stealthy as anyone I'd ever met. They shut the door quietly behind them and then glanced up at the ceiling.

"Lead the way, tiny bird," Ronan whispered.

Magic rippled along my raven wings as I slowly inched forward, flicking my ears to listen for any sign that anyone was ahead of us in the corridor. Tiarnan and Ronan were quiet with their swords held ready by their sides. Around the bend, I knew there were several bedrooms where warriors in training lived.

Our fight was not with them. We needed to find

Nemain instead. She wouldn't be on this floor, prowling around in the living quarters of the warriors.

She would likely be prowling around one of the floors above, holding meetings, giving orders, plotting murders. Or she might be down in the dungeons themselves, making the lives miserable of anyone she had captured. Through the gossip grapevine of the fae world, I hadn't heard any rumours about her taking new prisoners. But that did not mean she hadn't.

So, when we came to the foot of the stairs, I could either choose to go up or go down.

Up seemed the safest option. Going down into the dungeons might give us some insight into what Nemain had been up to these past few weeks, but it would also mean we could easily get trapped in narrow, dimly-lit pathways. The Fianna could easily sneak up behind us or lead us into a trap.

Wings beating heart against the stale air of the old mansion, I inched up further into the rafters, hoping my companions would understand what I meant to do.

But as soon as Ronan put a single foot on the bottom stair, arrows exploded out from both walls. An arrow grazed my wing, and I cried out in my raven's screech. Tiarnan dropped to the floor, unwounded but looking startled as hell. Ronan grunted, looking down at an arrow that had pierced him right in his stomach. My heart flipped over a million times. Blood oozed from the wound, painting his dark gray shirt a deep shade of red. He gasped for breath, clutching at the arrow that protruded out his back.

"I'm sorry, Clark," he said, his growl full of the pain he felt deep inside of his gut. "I know this is going to get us caught, but I have to shift. Otherwise, I'm going to die here. And I'm not going to let a bloody fae arrow be the end of me."

Fur began to sprout along Ronan's arms, his body shook. And in two seconds flat he had transferred into his wolf, a growling, snarling thing. The wound began to close up, the blood turning brown. Relief shuddered through my tiny body. It would take a few more shifts for his wound to fully heal, but he'd be fine.

"Well. Look what we've got here," a voice said from behind us.

I fluttered around to face him, finding half a dozen Fianna crowding into the thin corridor at the base of the stairs. With him was a human, one with dark brown hair trailing down to the floor. There was something haunted about her eyes, something I'd seen before. But I couldn't place it.

"Take them," one of the Fianna said. "Hurry, before they decide to fight."

The girl lifted her hands before her, and I realized what she was a second too late. A magical force slammed into me, knocking my raven body to the ground. Consciousness left me.

"Morrigan," a soft, scratchy voice drifted out from the darkness of the catacombs.

I twisted toward it, chills sweeping down my spine. I would recognize that voice anywhere, though I never would have expected it now.

"Nemain?" I called out my rival's name. My voice was clear and strong, despite the fear and doubt thumping through my

veins. The last time I'd seen Nemain, she had been standing against me. My guards had arrested her, taken her away to rot in the dungeons beneath the Primdark Castle in the north. Her imprisonment was to last until the day she died. It was impossible for her to be here now.

But here she was, stepping out of the shadows with her long dark hair drifting around her hollow face, making her look like a wraith from anyone's worst nightmares. Her teeth were yellowed when she flashed a strange smile, her nails long and crooked.

"Surprised to see me?" She hissed out a laugh. "You should know better, Morrigan. After all the times we've fought, you and me, and all the times you've pardoned me. You should know the only way to rid yourself of the threat of me...is with my death."

I shook my head, confused. She spoke of things I did not know. We had only fought once. I had never pardoned her before. And I certainly would not pardon her now.

I sucked in a breath, shook my head. "How are you here? How did you escape?"

She chuckled. "Escape is a funny word. It suggests that I slithered out of my dungeon and ran for my life, dodging arrows and swords and eyes. I did nothing of the sort. My guard let me out."

I blinked at her. "You're lying. That's impossible. None of my guards would have let you out of your dungeon."

"He is not your guard anymore."

The words roared in my ears, and my tongue thickened in my mouth. My worst nightmare, coming true. The world of fae had been fraught with war for so long. I'd long worried that my subjects would begin to turn on me, to desire something more than battles and blood. I did not blame them. I desired more myself.

But I would not let Nemain see my doubt, smell my fear. I

lifted my chin and made my voice as icy cold as her heart. "You know you can not beat me. Your powers may be great, but mine are greater."

Her yellow teeth flashed in the darkness. "That is why I did not come alone."

I woke up, screaming. And I knew without seeing the end of my dream that Nemain had won yet again. How many Morrigans had she defeated? Four, five, ten? Whatever the number was, I could not let it become a single one more.

4

My breath was ragged as I rolled onto my side in the dank, musty space. Flashes of the past filled my mind. The Morrigan, Nemain, legions of soldiers, rivers of blood. Even though the memories of the previous Morrigans had molded with my own, I still had these visions. There were hundreds of years to shift through, millions of tiny moments that fought for relevance in my mind. It was as if the deepest parts of me were bringing these specific memories to the forefront of all the noise.

My own mind was trying to tell me something.

What exactly was it trying to tell me? I had no freaking clue.

"She's alive," a familiar voice muttered from beside me. I flipped open my eyes to see Ronan staring down at me, a bored expression on his rugged face. He wore a scratchy blanket around his thick form, barely hiding the nakedness from his shift. "See, I told you there was nothing to worry about. It would take a hell of a lot more than a bloody sorcerer to take down our Morrigan."

Our Morrigan. My heart clenched tight. Ronan wasn't even a fae.

Frowning, I pushed up from the ground and glanced around. "I had a weird dream about Nemain again."

"That's great, Clark," Tiarnan said, gesturing at the thick metal bars that separated us from the rest of the world, including our future, our safety, and the lives of the fae we'd left behind at court. "But, in case you haven't noticed, we have more pressing issues to deal with. We've been caught by the bloody Fianna again."

"Sure," I said, wetting my lips. "But these dreams are important. I don't think I'd be having them if they weren't. And, based on my past visions, they're kind of timely. Whatever happened then could have a major impact on what happens now."

Tiarnan let out a hollow sigh and shook his head. "First, let's figure out how to get out of this hellhole, and then we can worry about your dreams."

My frown deepened. In any other situation, I'd have to agree with Tiarnan. Why worry about a dream when we were stuck inside a dungeon cell deep beneath the earth? Hell, there was a strong chance we'd never even get free.

But the visions had given me so much before…

In the distance, the door to the dungeon clanged open, and then slammed shut so hard that the sound echoed down the dingy corridor. I pressed up to my feet, heart hammering hard against my ribcage. Was it

Nemain? Had she come to put an end to our rivalry once and for all?

There had to be something inside my damn dream that could help me fight back one more time…this couldn't be the end. Not here. Deep within the heavy darkness of House Futrail.

But it wasn't Nemain at all who padded out of the shadows to stand before our jail cell. It was a frantic-eyed, bushy-haired fae whose breath came out from her painted lips in sharp bursts.

"Let me guess," Ronan said dryly. "You're here to take us to our execution."

"Nope." Her voice sounded strangled and sharp. "I've come here to let you out. There's a secret exit down that corridor."

Tiarnan blinked slowly. "Say what now?"

The fae let out a ragged breath as her eyes slid my way. "I've come to let you out. I don't agree with what Nemain is doing."

My heart flipped over itself, and I strode closer to the thick bars to peer into her tired, yellow eyes. "I'm sure a lot of Crimson Court fae don't agree with Nemain, even ones inside of House Futrail. But Nemain has her bond controlling every single one of you. The magic won't allow you to go against her orders."

Suspicion flooded through my veins like hot lava. Was this some sort of trap? A test? It didn't make much sense if it was. Nemain had already trapped us in this dungeon cell. What would be the point of making us believe a rogue fae wanted to help us escape, except to fuck with our minds?

"Nemain isn't here," the fae said in a hushed voice

before glancing over her shoulder at the shadowy corridor. "She's at the Ivory Court. She had Aed leak false information to you so that she could lure you here...and trap you in her dungeons. But, on the plus side, some of us have been able to pick out some loopholes in her orders. She wasn't here when the Fianna captured you. She has no idea you're here, yet."

Tiarnan's eyes went wide. "And because she doesn't know we're here yet, she hasn't made the order to keep us in this prison."

"Exactly," the strange fae said.

I nibbled on my lip. Every single cell in my body wanted to believe her. It might be our only chance at escape, at least one that didn't end with lots of blood puddles on the stone floor.

The only way to know for certain was to read her mind. Closing my eyes, I breathed the stale, mildewy air deep into my lungs and focused my mind on the fae who stood before us. Her energy was strong, vibrant, and bright compared to many of the minds I'd read since my life became entwined with the Crimson Court. Deep down in my bones, I knew without even listening in on a single thought that she was telling the truth. Her body hummed with purity. Still, I'd made the mistake of trusting without proof before, and I wouldn't make it again.

I hope the Morrigan sees that there are some of us on her side. The winning side. The rebellion against Nemain is growing. All we need is to be set free from our bond.

My eyes flew open, and I sucked in a sharp breath. Part relief, part hope, and part sorrow. I'd only known what it felt like to be bonded to one ruler—Balor. Despite my feelings for him, I'd hated it. I couldn't imagine what it was like to be bonded to someone tearing apart our world.

"Okay," I said with a nod, flicking my eyes to Tiarnan and Ronan. "She's telling the truth." I swept my eyes back to her face. "I just want to make one thing clear. No one knows you're helping us, right? If Nemain found out…"

I didn't need to finish that thought for every single one of us to know the end of it.

"Oh." Her eyes widened. "Some know my plans, but Nemain won't find out it was me."

Dread pooled in my gut. "You don't honestly believe that, do you? She'll make your friends tell her how we escaped. They won't have another choice."

"We have a plan. We're going to make it seem like you were never here."

I arched a brow. "That's only going to work if all those Fianna are part of your rebellion, as you call it."

"The warriors only saw a bird." She shrugged. "They thought it was you, but it wasn't. Ronan and Tiarnan used a fake bird as a distraction. She might buy it, you know…Plus, hardly anyone knows about the secret exit, so no one will see you escape."

I crossed my arms over my chest, heart hammering hard. I had a bad feeling I wasn't going to like where this whole thing was going. "And how will you explain how Ronan and Tiarnan got out of here?"

She grimaced. "I won't be letting them escape. To make this work, they have to stay here."

A beat passed in tense silence. Suddenly, Ronan clapped his strong hand onto my shoulder and squeezed tight. "Don't worry about us, Clark. Get yourself out of here and save the fae."

I kept my expression blank, and my body relaxed, so as not to reveal just how hard my heart slammed against my ribcage. Obviously, I wanted out of here. Hell, I *needed* to get out of here. And I knew Ronan and Tiarnan could take care of themselves. They'd both gotten out of far stickier situations than this one.

"Okay," I said, voice calm and clear. My eyes locked with the fae's. I couldn't bear to look at either of my boys, not like this, not when I was leaving them behind.

Relief flickered across the fae's face, and her whole chest rose as she sucked in a breath. "Thank the Morrigan. For a second there, I thought you'd stay locked up in this dungeon. We'll never break free of Nemain if you do."

"You're welcome."

"Oh. *Thank the Morrigan.*" Her cheeks went pink. "That's right. You're her. Or she's you. It's easy to forget…you just look so normal."

I gave her a tight smile. "Trust me, I'm aware."

Her cheeks darkened even more, and she fumbled with the lock on the cell. The door swung open wide, the hinges creaking against the eerie stone walls. I took a deep breath and stepped outside, still giving the fae my tight smile as she hastily shut the door behind me, trapping my boys inside, once again.

"I'm sorry," I said to her back.

She whirled to face me after locking the cell door. "Sorry? Why would you be sorry? It's not your fault you were reincarnated into a half-fae."

"That's not what I'm sorry for."

With a deep breath, I slammed my palm against her forehead. Magic hurtled out of me and into her.

Her eyelids fluttered. Her lips parted in a gasp. And then she fell to the floor.

I didn't wait even a single beat. I knelt beside her and grabbed the keys that had fallen from her slack fingers. Two seconds later, I had the door back open and my boys out in the dungeon hall on either side of me. They blinked down at our saviour, expressions screwed up by their tortured emotions.

"What the hell did you do to her, Clark?" Tiarnan whispered.

"I just knocked her out." I shrugged. "She'll sleep soundly for a few hours, and then she'll be back to normal. No damage at all."

Ronan arched a brow. "New weapon in your arsenal?"

I tapped my head. "I have a couple of tricks up my sleeve, thanks to the memories of all the Morrigans. I was hoping I wouldn't have to use this one so soon, especially not on her. But I wasn't about to leave you two here to face Nemain's wrath alone. I don't think that little story about the bird is going to work."

Ronan frowned. "No, I didn't think so either, but what are we going to do about this female? It'll be pretty clear what happened when the Fianna find her here, and our cell empty."

I gave him a grim smile. "We're going to have to take her with us."

5

My little spell didn't exactly go as planned. The fae from House Futrail should have been knocked out for hours. Instead, she woke up only moments later, limbs flailing, eyes rolling back in her head.

Ronan and Tiarnan wrestled her into the car after we stole out the back way.

"What the hell!" Ronan exclaimed when the fae sunk her teeth into his bicep and bit so hard that blood poured from the tiny, incisor-shaped wounds.

She snarled and growled, but pulled back in a snap, as if she'd been slapped. Her words came out in a rush. "I'm so sorry. I can't stop myself. It's the bond. Nemain made an order. We can never leave, not unless she gives us permission."

And with that, her mouth was latched right back onto Ronan's arm again.

He growled, his lips curling around his teeth, eyes bleeding yellow.

"Ronan," I warned, even knowing that he couldn't

help himself. Caught in between a stranger's teeth, the wolf within him was no doubt scratching to get out. It wanted to fight back. It wanted blood for itself.

Tiarnan glanced up, frustration painting his features. He was trying—and failing—to get her buckled into the car. "A little help here, Clark?"

"Sorry, it didn't really work last time."

"It worked for five minutes. That's all we need."

And so I slammed my palm against her forehead again. This time, I felt a little guilty about it.

~

"Clark, you're going to have to swap places with me," Ronan growled from the backseat. We were halfway back to the Crimson Court, and our fae—who we now knew as Lizzie, had woken up from my fail of a magic spell at least seven times. Ronan was stuck in the back with her, and his arm showed the proof.

I twisted in my seat and frowned back at where she thrashed against the seatbelt. "I timed that one. Thirty seconds. The one before that was about forty-five. Her time out is getting shorter and shorter, like the magic is getting weaker. I clearly don't have a good handle on this spell. If I keep trying it, we're going to end up with zero seconds. Why not save it for when we really need it? For some kind of emergency?"

Ronan glowered at me just as Lizzie grabbed his arm and wrapped her mouth around it. "I guess you don't see me losing my arm as an emergency. Got it. Thanks for nothing, love."

"I mean, you could just knock her out the old-fashioned way," I said.

"Go ahead," Lizzie said around a mouthful of Ronan's arm, chest heaving. "I'll understand if that's what you have to do."

He turned to glower at the fae beside him. But then he sighed, shook his head, even though her teeth still dug into his skin. "Just drive faster. Get us back to London." He snorted. "Never thought I'd ever be the one to say that."

~

But things did not improve once we were back in London. The three of us barely managed to carry Lizzie through the back entrance of the Court—we figured letting the protesting humans see us abducting someone probably wasn't the greatest plan—kicking, flailing, and generally screaming bloody murder.

Once we made it to the command station, Moira rushed off to find Balor while we strapped Lizzie to a chair and stuffed a sock in her mouth. Kyle gave us the sock. I could only pray to the unknown fae gods that it was clean.

I felt his power before I heard or saw anything else. It billowed into the room like a force of nature. It took my breath away every time. There was something about it, something I wasn't certain if anyone else could feel but me. Darkness and power and pure magic. I wondered if he felt the same just before I walked into a room.

Balor took one look at the trapped, abducted fae

and turned on me. "I told Moira she was wrong. That you had not taken it upon yourself to abduct one of Nemain's clearly devoted subjects. You wouldn't be dumb enough, or careless enough, to do such a thing."

My skin prickled, both from anger and from the magical bond that pushed and pulled us together, over and over again across centuries. "Lower your voice, Balor," I said in a warning, hoping to remind him of the position I held now, without being forced to say it out loud in front of all the others.

He blinked at me, and then let out a harsh laugh. Bowing down low, he growled. "Of course, my Queen. How could I forget? You haven't just stolen my throne and taken all my fae away from me, fae I've spent decades upon decades protecting, against all costs."

His words hit me like a fist in the gut. I stumbled back, heart racing. I'd known he hadn't been thrilled about me taking his crimson throne, but he'd never given any indication that he was *angry* about it. In fact, he'd been the first to kneel in front of me.

A little warning bell rang in the back of my mind. Me and Balor. Balor and me. Forever entwined throughout history. Sometimes lovers. Sometimes mortal enemies that went to extreme lengths to destroy each other. Balor had told me fate had given us love this time. But had it? No matter what we did, or how many times we came together, we kept finding ourselves at odds.

Under the sway of my step-father's magic, I had followed Nemain's orders and helped her kill Balor's sister. Was that the moment our fate had been sealed?

"I'm going to ignore that," I said, my voice dropping several octaves past what I'd even known was possible. Magic radiated from my own skin, filling up the room in a way it never had before. "You've been through a lot, and giving up your throne was a huge ask, especially after Fionn tried to steal it from you, and then Nemain took it for her own. But this infighting… we cannot have it if this Court is going to survive."

Power pulsed against my skin, an intoxicating magic that threatened to drag me deep into darkness. Wind swirled through the command station, bringing with it the stench of ash and death. Shadows surrounded us, and clouds of mist swept from one end of the room to the next. Somewhere in the distance, a familiar voice shouted my name.

It was enough to break the spell.

My hands dropped to my sides, and with it, my magic. Instantly, the shadows vanished, but the unease, the darkness, and the danger still remained, deep inside my gut.

"Right." Moira stepped between us, frowned at me, and then at Balor. "Whatever this is, you need to sort it out. And fast. You're the two most powerful fae we have in this Court, and you can't even be in the same room together right now. We're never going to win this war if you keep…doing whatever it is you're doing. After we figure out what we're doing with our bloody hostage, you need to go have a cuppa and sort your shit out. Got it?"

I stared at Moira, my lips twitching. If she were anyone else in the world, I probably would have snapped back.

But it was Moira. And I agreed with her, wholeheartedly.

"Sounds good to me," I said with a nod.

"Good." She turned toward Balor, arms crossed firmly over her chest. Her eyebrows winged upward. "Well?"

He was still glowering as much as he'd been since the moment he stepped foot inside the command station. "I cannot promise we'll come to some sort of resolution."

"Well, you bloody well try." Moira rolled her eyes and whirled back to our friendly neighborhood abductee, who had been watching the entire exchange with wide, curious eyes. If she were some kind of hidden, undercover spy for Nemain, we'd really ruined it now. If Nemain found out just how deep the discord in this Court went, she'd use it for all it was worth.

"So, what are we thinking?" Kyle asked after clearing his throat. He edged in beside us, knelt down, and peered into Lizzie's eyes. She stilled in her thrashing, eyeing him curiously right back.

"She has been extremely hostile and violent since we took her off the grounds of House Futrail when she was nothing but compliant and helpful, almost eagerly so, before that." I sighed and shook my head. "It's impossible to know how much of this is controlled by Nemain and how much of this is voluntary."

Lizzie's lips moved, her words coming out in muffled murmurs around the sock.

"Should we let her speak?" Moira asked with a frown.

"No," I said in unison with Balor. I shot a glance

his way and caught his eyes. For a moment, things felt normal. We were in sync, we worked as a team. But then the clouded history swept back in again, darkening what we had now.

I cleared my throat to clarify. "I'm not sure how much we could trust. If Nemain has ordered her to violently resist leaving the House, then she will have likely fed her some lines to say to any captor. I'm going to have to read her mind again."

This time, there was a little more resistance. Likely Nemain's doing. There had been no barriers before, but we weren't working within the constraints of Nemain's orders. Probably. It certainly didn't seem like this fae was faking her repeated flailing attempts to get free, due to Nemain's orders.

Her thoughts rushed by me so fast that it was difficult to pick out the one that would help us. I cleared my throat, all I could manage in my zoned out state inside someone else's mind. But Tiarnan got the hint. He'd seen me in action like this before.

In the distance, down a deep dark well, I could hear his muffled voice as he asked the question we were dying to know.

"Are you working with Nemain?" he asked.

Depends on how you define working, she thought. *She's given me orders I'm forced to follow. But I choose to go against her when I can.*

I let out an exhale of relief. Still not ideal, but the best case scenario out of many terrible options.

"Is there anything you can tell us about what she's up to right now?" Ronan cut in, his growly voice even deeper through the muddled mind of Lizzie.

A beat passed before I could latch onto any

thought. Hesitation flickered through her mind, almost as though she wasn't sure of what she knew. *Nemain has gone to the Ivory Court to get them to her side.*

She must have said the words out loud, too, because Tiarnan asked another question immediately. "Why would she be willing to leave London when Clark is inside the Court and sitting on the throne? Wouldn't she want to invade first?"

Nemain is biding her time. She is counting on a new prophecy, one that will win the war for Faerie. One about the Morrigan and the Smiter.

"What prophecy?" Moira's voice went sharp. "Where did she hear this?"

From the Goddess of Prophecies and Dreams.

"From Caer," she said aloud.

My heart thumped. This must have been the same prophecy we'd already heard, the one about Balor's child stabbing him right in the heart.

This is a new one and an ancient one at the same time. It has to do with their magic. The one that shatters glass.

All the blood drained from my face as I snapped my mind out of Lizzie's thoughts. I glanced from Tiarnan's shocked eyes to Ronan's furrowed brows to Moira's parted lips. My own face must have looked as shocked as theirs. This was not the same prophecy at all.

This was another one. I finally turned to Balor and stared into his orange-red eye. It had to do with our bond.

6

I strode into the elaborate flat that had become my own when the crown had shifted from Balor's head to mine. Kicking off my shoes, I padded straight over to the bar in my socked feet and poured myself a soothing mixture of gin and tonic. My bones were weary, and so was my heart. It had been a long day, and it still wasn't over.

With a deep breath, I swirled my drink and edged closer to the floor-to-ceiling window that looked out onto the sparkling London night. Out there, danger lurked. Humans were plotting against us, the vampires were doing who knew what, and Nemain weaved strand after strand, hoping to stop us once and for all.

In here, things weren't much better. I spun on my heels to face Balor, who had followed me up the stairs and into the penthouse. He stood just in the archway that separated the living area from the kitchen, his hands slung into his pockets. His hair was in disarray, his eyes dark and hollow.

"I don't like fighting with you," he said tiredly. "It's the last thing in the world I want to do."

"Then, why do you keep fighting me?" I asked in a voice so quiet that it barely whispered across the space.

"I can't help it." He took a step into the room, his feet brushing against the hardwood. "I am fine one moment, and then I am not. I just get so frustrated, so angry."

My heart pulsed. "At me?"

"No." He shook his head and shrugged. "Yes, but no. The anger isn't logical. It isn't real."

"It sure feels real, Balor."

"And what do *you* feel?" he prompted. "The arguments aren't one-sided here, Clark."

A flicker of irritation went through me, but I doused it fast. "Annoyance. Frustration." I took a step away from the window, toward the most powerful fae I'd ever met. "Yearning."

His entire body shuddered as he locked his eye with mine. "It was never like this with any of the others. Was it?"

He meant the prior Smiters, the previous Morrigans. We weren't the first, and we wouldn't be the last. Not when this vicious cycle of reincarnation happened time after time after time again. One day we would both die at the hands of our enemies. And another Morrigan would take my place. I just hoped she was better at this whole thing than I was.

"No, it wasn't," I said quietly. "They never went through this push and pull. They either hated each other from the very start, or they fell in love."

He nodded. "There was either push, or there was

pull. None of the others experienced this fucking whiplash."

I pressed my lips firmly together. The last thing in the world I wanted was to lose Balor Beimnech because the magic of the bond was too much for us to handle. We'd been through a lot, even before we'd even met. To think we'd gotten past all that, to think we'd been able to find each other despite all the odds, it made me want to believe that we were destined for something good.

"Maybe we can find a way," I said softly, reaching toward him and placing my palms flat on his muscular chest. "We've seen each other now for who we really are. None of the past versions of ourselves have been able to do that. Maybe it's enough for us to rise above the flip of the coin. We found a loophole for Caer's prophecy about your son. We can find a way out of this one, too."

Balor's eye sparked with fire as he dropped his lips to mine and kissed me more deeply than he ever had before. Sparks lit up along my skin, causing my entire body to transform into flames.

Breathless, I pulled away and dropped my forehead to his chest, breathing so heavily my breath fogged on his shirt. "Are you sure we should do this, Balor?"

"I've never been more certain of anything in my life." His voice went rough as he dragged his fingers down my back. My spine curved in response, and I shuddered. "I need you, Clark. When I'm not with you, a part of me feels dead."

I wrapped my arms around him, everything within me understanding exactly what he meant. With the bond, with our shared past, my soul was linked to his.

"What about our fighting?" I whispered. "No matter what we say or do, it feels like we can't stop ourselves from hurling insults."

"We will do like you said." He twined his fingers through my hair. "We will rise above it. We will move past it. The love I feel for you is real, Clark. It's the most real thing I've ever experienced in my life. I won't let this magic rip you away from me."

It was everything I wanted to hear and more. Finally, as if expelling a very long held breath, I relaxed against him and let go of all my worries. The two of us together were a hurricane. Nothing could stop us. Not even an ancient bond that yearned to tear us apart.

I leaned into him and breathed in his intoxicating scent. Dropping back my head, I looked up into his face. That gleaming orange eye rippled with the very same desire churning through my core. I reached up and pushed at the eye patch, but he caught my hand before I could pull it away.

"Not tonight," he said in a low growl. "I want you to see me as Balor, the strong powerful fae you first met. Not the one who lost his power to a false Queen."

"You are that same Balor to me, with or without your flaming eye."

"Just not tonight." He pressed his lips against mine. "Tonight, I don't want the focus to be on my eye."

I wanted to argue with him, yet again. I'd seen his hollow black eye, and I had loved him even more for it. He didn't need to hide it from me any longer. But tonight, I vowed we would no longer fight. And if he did not wish to take his patch off tonight, then so be it.

I slipped my hands down his face and smiled. "Very well. You win this time."

He let out a low chuckle. "That might be the only time you've ever said those words to me."

"Don't get used to it."

His expression sobered. "What do you think about Lizzie's words, and Caer's new prophecy."

I squeezed my eyes tight. "To be honest, I really don't want to think about that right now. Caer's prophecies are never good things."

"You need to go to her, to Caer." He slid his thumb beneath my chin and caressed my skin. "I will go with you if you'd like."

"Balor," I murmured, looking up at him with half-lidded eyes. "No more talk about prophecies and magic and pain. Not tonight. Not now."

He understood what I meant without needing me to say more. With a wicked smile, he lifted me from the floor. I wrapped my thighs around his waist and clung to his body. Everything suddenly felt right once again. We were together, him and I, and we would not let anything tear us apart.

When we reached the bedroom, I expected him to drop me back onto the bed, but he lowered me to the floor instead. My bum brushed against the hardwood floor as my back arched. Staring up into his orange eye, the bond between us wrapped around my heart. It felt like a physical link. Like it was anchored deep within my soul, and attached to a cord that stretched across the space between us, the other end wrapped tightly around his own soul. Logically, I knew it was only magic. But that did not make it seem any less real.

Balor growled, leaning down to nip at my earlobe. I loved it when he did that. It made sparks dance across every inch of my skin, and desire swirl through my veins. My need grew as he continued to bite. Wetting my lips, I dragged my hands across his chest and lifted his shirt over his head.

His body was unlike anything I'd ever seen. Everything about him screamed *fae*. It would be impossible for anyone to think he was anything but one of the most powerful supernatural creatures alive. My fingers dipped along his corded muscles as I drank in every inch of his skin. Everything about him made me feel breathless.

It wasn't how perfectly he was built. It wasn't the six-pack abs or the bulging biceps. It was the strength, the pure power. It radiated off his body in waves, washing over me and begging me to give in, to drown in it.

And I wanted to drown.

Balor saw the need in my eyes and pulled my clothing off my body in one fluid motion. He smiled, and then danced his tongue along my throat. I shuddered beneath him, spreading open my legs and pressing my core against him.

"Someone is eager," he murmured as he continued to massage my neck with his mouth and tongue. I moaned, my eyelids fluttering a million beats a minute.

The magic that pulled between us grew, and strands of white hot electricity slithered in the air behind Baylor's head. I widened my eyes, but for once, I wasn't afraid. There were no swirling shadows, there was no darkness. This magic felt pure.

"I'm always eager for you," I whispered.

He smiled and began to drift lower. "Don't make promises you can't keep."

"Trust me," I said in a gasp as his mouth curled around my peaked nipple. "Of all the promises I've ever made, this is the one I would put above all the rest."

I meant every word. Every time he touched me, I wanted more. Every time he looked at me, my need became so great that I could barely think of anything else. When he was in another room, I could feel his magic curling around my face seductively. Even with miles between us, I couldn't get him out of my head. The bond was always there, linking us, making me want to do anything I could to get to him.

Balor had dug himself deep into my heart, and I could not imagine him never being there.

His face dipped between my spread thighs. I let out a gasp at the soft flutter of his tongue dragging against the very core of me. My fingernails dug into the hardwood, leaving moon-shaped indents of my fingernails behind. He was going to drive me crazy, teasing me like this. He knew it, too. He liked to see me squirm, bare and open before him. Nothing stood between us anymore.

We had danced outside the bounds of the prophecy. We had found a loophole, one that would mean we would never have to hold back. But then that strange magic of our bond had begun to pull us away from each other once again.

We could not let the magic destroy us.

Pleasure built up within me, drowning out everything else. I reached down and slid my fingers between the thick strands of his hair, holding on tight as he took me to the very edge. Just before I crashed onto those beautiful shores of satisfaction, Balor pulled back and smiled.

I was aching on the floor, desperate for him. "You're terrible."

He started to climb toward me, his body hovering over mine. A wicked smile spread across his lips. "Am I? Well, if you really believe I'm terrible, then maybe I should just go to bed."

"Don't you dare," I growled, wrapping my legs around his bum and pulling him against my hips.

"That's what I thought." And then his voice went rough. He took my face in his palm, leaned down, and breathed me in. "I love you, Clark."

The words came out a whisper. "I love you, too."

Gently, he pressed his length inside of me. He groaned, and my body shuddered against his. He had left me so aching and ready for him that it wouldn't be long before I fell over the edge of that high but blissful cliff.

He rocked against me, our bodies linking as the bond snapped tight. Magic whorled around us now, the fiery strands whipping through the air and creating a hot breeze that blew Balor's hair away from his face.

He grabbed my arms, pinning my wrists to the ground. A delicious thrill went through me. Pleasure built. Hot fire shot through every cell in my body. I couldn't think. I couldn't breathe. All I needed was him.

Just as Balor groaned with the final release of his own pleasure, I found myself hurtled over the cliff. Magic shot out from our bodies, slamming into the walls. The floor-to-ceiling windows that looked over London shattered into a million tiny pieces. The explosion rocked the entire floor, pieces of broken glass raining down all around us. Balor curled his body over mine, protecting me from the onslaught of the shards.

"What just happened?" He asked in a rough voice as he stared at the carnage that surrounded us.

My heart thumped hard. "I think our bond just shattered the Court."

"Morrigan," the smiter said.

A beat passed before I could bring myself to speak. "Smiter. Why are you here?"

"I have come because the power of Faerie is drawing me to you. I cannot hold myself back any longer."

Pushing up from the throne, I strode to the edge of the stone dais and frowned down at one of my biggest threats. He was part of my Court, but I knew he worked against me. I had seen him conspiring in the corners with Nemain. But perhaps it was for the best not to show him just how much I knew.

"I feel the same." I flicked my gaze at my two guards and gave them a nod. They hesitated for a moment, but then disappeared out of view. "I want nothing more than for us to be together, but you must understand my position. I cannot marry one of my own warriors."

Disdain flickered across the Smiter's face, his true emotions coming to life behind his pleasant smile, but only for a fleeting moment. "I thought you were above valuing position over all else."

"I do not value position. However, I do value how my actions are perceived by the wider fae world."

"I see." He stood from where he knelt before me and pulled a knife from his belt. "I did not truly expect you to accept my offer. I thought it would come to this."

Magic swarmed around me as I curled my hands into fists and rolled back my shoulders. "So, this was not a marriage proposal after all. I wish I could say I'm surprised, but I am not."

"Oh, it was a marriage proposal, dear Queen," he said with a snarl. "If you had accepted, I would have wed you and slowly wrestled control of the fae from you to me. Kings are far more valued in this human realm than Queens. And if you didn't accept? Then, I would kill you."

Pain flickered through my heart. It was not the worst betrayal I had ever endured as my time leading the fae, but it cut deeper than the rest. There was something about the Smiter that did truly draw me to him, and I respected his power and strength. Above all that, I did not like harming my own fae, even one pulling a knife on me.

Before he could launch his attack, I opened my mouth and screamed. Power radiated from my parted lips and slammed hard against the Smiter's chest. He collapsed to the floor immediately, and my guards rushed in from the wings.

My most-trusted knight knelt beside him and looked up at me. "What shall we do with him, my Queen?"

"Take him to the dungeons and prepare him for execution. He has committed treason here this night."

7

It was hard to pretend like nothing had happened. Down in the command station, it was all anyone could talk about. Or, at least that was what it sounded like as I strode down the hallway to the chorus of gossipy voices. They all fell to a hush when I walked into the room, and they cast their eyes downward.

I pursed my lips. "Don't stop on my account."

"Sorry, Clark," Moira said without letting a single beat pass. "We all heard the explosion. Figured it had something to do with you and Balor, but we didn't want to interrupt…" She arched her brow, leaving the question unasked.

I glanced from her, to Kyle, to Elise. "Don't tell me you think I tried to kill him."

"Of course not," Elise said, rushing over. "But we've all seen the magic. We know what it can do. Plus, we all heard the prophecy thing about shattering glass. Is he…is he okay?"

"He's fine," I snapped. "We weren't even fighting

when it happened. We were—" I cleared my throat, and every single pair of eyes widened. Shit, I'd said too much. But it wasn't as if my relationship with Balor was a secret. Everyone knew about us. No sense hiding that we'd somewhat reconciled.

Until I'd had that dream, of course. Even amidst all the memories of our past lives, I hadn't fully witnessed what our wrath toward each other was like. The hate. The violence. I shuddered, squeezing my fists tight. He had tried to kill me in one of our past lives. More than many, if my flickering memories were any indication.

And I had ordered his execution.

The dream had stopped before he'd died, but I still had access to the truth. Two weeks later, a filthy, weakening Smiter had been brought to the guillotine, and the Court had executed him in front of hundreds of fae.

He'd ranted and raved about his fiery eye up until the very end. If he'd been able to use it, he would have. My knights had forced a contraption on his head, one that prevented him from using his power.

I couldn't imagine what it would take to turn us against each other like that. Not now. Not in this life.

The crown, maybe? But neither of us were that hungry for power. I wouldn't kill him for the throne, and he wouldn't kill me. Nemain wasn't whispering to him in back corners, garnering his loyalty to her side.

So, our fate wouldn't land on that. It *couldn't*.

Balor and I would never plot to kill the other.

"Long story short, our magic got out of control, but both of us are fine." I pressed my lips firmly together. "Now, let's move on to something else, shall

ALL'S FAE IN LOVE AND WAR

we? Today's tasks are a good start. I need you all to keep trying to get information out of Lizzie while I take care of a few things."

Elise arched a silver brow. "What kind of things?"

"I'm going to see Caer," I said. "If Nemain is in possession of some information, then we need it, too. I don't like feeling as if we're not on a level playing field."

Moira snorted. "We're never going be on a level playing field with that one. She doesn't operate like we do. She's got her own rules. Hell, she's got her own damn game."

I totally agreed with Moira, but I shot her a mock glare all the same. "We at least have to try."

"I'm guessing Balor isn't going with you this time either?" Ronan asked from where he observed the meeting, arms crossed in the corner.

"After our little shattering glass thing, that is a big no from me." It pained me to say it. This prophecy involved my mate, too. But I didn't even want to tell him I was going, for fear he'd insist on coming along. We'd never be able to make the drive there and back without breaking the whole damn car.

"I'd volunteer to go with you, tiny bird, but I don't much like that kind of magic," Ronan said.

"I'll go," Tiarnan said. "I've met her before. She's intense, sure, but I don't mind her."

"No," I said, cutting in, eyes falling shut. "This is something I need to take care of myself."

Every mouth in the room opened to argue, but I shut them up with the firm glare I shot around the room. Even though Nemain controlled the bond, every fae in the command station looked to me as

Queen. Because I was the Morrigan. It meant I got a teensy bit more respect than I did when I was merely Clark Cavanaugh, half-fae, half-shifter.

Just a teensy bit though. If they *really* disagreed with me, they had no bones about making their opinions known.

I hoped that never changed.

I never wanted to be the kind of ruler that shut down opposing views. The fae of the Crimson Court, and the rest of Faerie as a whole, would have the freedom to make their own choices, so long as they didn't harm anyone else. I didn't want to control anyone. I just wanted to make sure everyone stayed safe.

"So, what do you need from us?" Moira asked.

With a nod, I gave each of them their duties for the day. Tasks that would keep the Court ticking along and the fae safe inside of it. We didn't want anyone accepting strange phone calls or leaving the premises. If they did, Nemain would be able to get to them. She might not be in London, but she would no doubt have her lackeys, like Aed, out and about, trying to whisper orders into pointed fae ears.

After I'd doled out everyone's daily tasks, I strode out of the command station to head to the bank of cars Balor kept hidden deep within the Court grounds. When I was halfway down the hall, footsteps echoed behind me. I turned to find Tiarnan jogging to catch up.

"I thought you might have forgotten," he said, breath puffing. "Caer likes presents."

Memories flickered in my mind. Back when he and I had first gone to Caer, he'd taken a secretive little box to her, in order to encourage her to talk to us. I shuddered, remembering. Whatever was inside of that box, I'd had a sneaking suspicion it was something pretty damn grim. Like a finger.

"I don't have time to track down something creepy to give to her. Not when Nemain is at the Ivory Court, wooing new friends."

He grinned. "You might find this a little strange, but I actually keep a few things around just in case I ever need to give a goddess a gift."

I arched a brow. "Not a *little* strange, Tiarnan. A *lot* strange."

"Make fun all you want, but you need me now," he continued, smiling. "So, what do you say? Want me to go to my room and grab one for you?"

I wanted to roll my eyes and say no, but...he had a point. It would be a complete waste of time for me to drive all the way to the Lake of the Dragon Mouth just for Caer to turn me away because I'd forgotten a piece of skin to gift her. With a sigh, I nodded and followed Tiarnan up to his room.

I was surprised when I got a good look inside of it. He'd settled in these past few weeks, and he'd filled up the space with his collections, ranging from old textbooks on battle strategies to tiny wooden carvings of ravens. He'd framed and hung replicas of Van Gogh's greatest highlights, as well as a gothic photograph of the old West Norwood Catacombs.

"Wow," I said, staring at the old photograph. "You've really made this place your home, even though you're just crashing here."

He passed me another little box identical to the

one we'd had the first time we visited Caer. It was tied up with a little ribbon. I didn't look inside.

"That's actually something I wanted to talk to you about," he said. "I don't really want to crash here anymore."

I cocked my head and frowned. "You want to move out? Where will you go? Ronan's?"

"No, that's not what I mean." He took my hands in his and knelt before me. When he looked up, his gaze was piercing and raw and full of pure devotion. "When Fionn kicked me out, I became a solitary fae. You're my Queen, and I want to serve you. Properly. I want to be inducted back into the Crimson Court, and I want to make this House my home."

I blinked at him. "You do? But what about the Fianna? What about your old House?"

"I can't go back there," he said quietly. "Not as long as Nemain still rules."

Tiarnan strode over to his wastebasket and held up beer can after beer can after beer can. "I've been dealing with my past the only way I knew how. Drinking. Every single damn day. I thought it would drown out the loneliness I felt at being a solitary fae, but it's done nothing of the sort. Hell, part of the reason I haven't asked you if I could come back into the fold is because I was sure you'd say no. I was the male who betrayed you after all. I thought all those horrible things about your kind. Things I wish I could erase from my mind. Poison."

I couldn't lie and tell him I hadn't noticed the drinking. He'd been at Ronan's almost every night. The shifter loved a good beer, but he never drank so much he passed out. And with Tiarnan's metabolism, he shouldn't either, but he'd been drowning himself in the booze.

With a soft smile, I crossed the room and placed a hand on his shoulder. I'd forgiven him for all the poison Fionn had leaked into his mind a long time ago. "I would be honoured to have you back in the Court."

He blinked at me. "Do you mean that, Clark?"

"I do. Unfortunately, it's going to have to wait." I gave him a sad smile. "I don't hold that power. Nemain does. But I promise you, Tiarnan. I give you my word. You will be part of this Court again."

Of course, I didn't really plan for this Court to remain as it was, not anymore. I'd been thinking long and hard about this for awhile. Faerie should be one again. The fae should come together instead of being apart. I pressed Tiarnan's gift back into his hands, a better idea forming in my mind.

I would take a gift to Caer. One that would change the course of this entire war.

8

*R*ain tore down from the cloudy skies as I parked along the ridge deep within the forests of Devon. Shivers coursed along my skin as the temperature dropped from chilly to worse. I shrugged on a jacket and dipped my feet into wellies before popping out of the car. Tall trees trembled in the rain-soaked skies, and clouds scuttled around a moon shaped like a torn fingernail.

Everything was just as it had been the first time I'd come here, minus Tiarnan.

This meeting with Caer…it was something I had to do on my own.

I trudged up the hillside, through thick brush and towering trees, shivering as large splats of rain fell onto my head. Caer lived just on the edge of The Lake of the Dragon's Mouth, a magical little valley hidden deep within these woods. I wondered if any humans had ever stumbled upon the place, and what they would have seen if they had.

And if Caer would have let them go without bother…

When I came to the edge of the clearing, I stepped out from the trees and into beautiful beaming sunshine. The hills were dotted with flowers in every shade imaginable: silver, aqua, and marigold. The glowing orb of rippling water sat in the very midst of it all, fish darting just below the surface. Suddenly, warmth swept across me, drying me instantly from head to toe. I shrugged off my jacket and left it beside a rock, letting the sunbeams sink into my skin.

Down below, in the wide expanse of brilliant green, something stirred. I glanced down, and there she was. The ancient goddess of prophecy and dreams scurried out of her little grass hut, one without a roof. She stared up at me with those hollow dark eyes that saw deep into my soul.

I shivered and went down.

When I reached the valley of the hill, she stood waiting for me in a black gown that whispered behind her, flickering in a breeze I neither felt nor saw anywhere else. The trees all around us were still, the leaves on bushes didn't move.

"I have been waiting for you to return." She handed me a lopsided brown mug of something that steamed from the top. "You have questions for me, but what will you give me in return?"

I took the mug from her withering hands and took a sip of the hot liquid. After the rain and the smog, I gratefully drank it dry. Then, she held out her hands, expectantly. Last time we'd come, Tiarnan had brought her a gift. Thankfully, he'd reminded me.

After handing back her mug, I dug into my bag and pulled a small wrapped box from deep within it.

"What is this delicious thing?" She reached for it, greedily, and peered inside. Her eyes tripped across the glinting metal, and she frowned. "I did not foresee this." A frown dragged down the corners of her eyes. "Are you playing with me, Morrigan?"

"No, I am not," I said, pushing the box into her hands. "This is the Crimson Court crown, and it is yours now, to use however you wish. There is magic within it. You could extract it and use it for something else."

Her gaze was piercing. "You are the Morrigan. The crown is yours. Why have you not claimed it?"

I sucked in a deep breath. This part was a gamble. Caer's political allegiances had always been shifting sand. As the times changed, so did she, if she thought it was to her benefit. By making my stance known to her now, I would be revealing my plans. Plans she might not agree with. Plans that might prevent her from revealing the prophecy to me.

She had revealed it to Nemain, after all.

"I intend to do away with the separate Courts, to unite the fae together. No more bonds with Princes and Princesses. There will be one Queen, and the fae of the world will be free to make their own decisions."

Her eyes flashed. "Interesting that your goal is not far different than your enemy's."

"You mean, Nemain?" I cocked a brow. "Our goals are nothing alike. She intends to use the bonds to maximum effect. She already is."

"You both wish to unite Faerie once again, after

decades spent as separate Courts. In that, you are the same."

I frowned. "Sure, but method matters. The ends don't justify the means. Controlling people to get what you want is pretty much the opposite of what I want to do."

Caer reached out a single, long, withering finger and placed it against my chest. "The Morrigan may not use the ruling bonds, but do not forget the rest of Faerie does. You can make change happen, but you cannot do so without respect. Such as toward your Balor, who used the bond himself."

"What are you trying to say, Caer?"

"I wish Faerie to be reunited once again. That is why I shared the prophecy with Nemain, and it is why I will share it with you now. But be warned. Understanding the truth will not be as easy as you would like it to be. You must take a journey into the past in order to see the future."

"That sounds a lot like the last prophecy you told me."

She nodded, gravely. "Oh, yes. It certainly is. You accepted your past, and now the memories of prior Morrigans have merged with your own. That information is priceless. However, it is quite a different thing to remember and quite another to experience it for yourself."

My frown deepened. "I don't understand."

She trailed past me to stand on the edge of the bank, her deep, sorrowful eyes cast down toward the water. "The Lake of the Dragon's Mouth. You know what it is, yes?"

I nodded, even though I hadn't realised until now

that I *did* in fact know, through past memories from other Morrigans. "It's a magical well, leading far back into the past."

"It is the portal that originally brought us to this mortal realm. Faerie was destroyed, and the fae were forced to find another world in which to live. We found this one."

Strange memories echoed deep inside my mind, but the thoughts were muddled, the images were blurred. "I was there. I think. It's so far in the past that it's hard for me to see it."

She nodded once again. "You were there, and I was there, too. Baleros, the original smiter, appeared in your life for the very first time. Back then, in Faerie, when your family ruled without question. The Morrigan, Princess of them all."

My mouth went dry at the strange, dark tone her voice had taken on. Everything she said had a ring of truth about it, even though the memories were too murky for me to see. "Why can't I remember that? I thought I'd broken through the barriers that kept the memories from view?"

"They happened in Faerie. Not here. The magic cannot travel through realms. None can." She pointed down at the lake. "You must return through the portal if you wish to know the full truth of your past."

I swallowed hard. "I thought fae had tried to dive into this lake before, and every single time, they died."

"They were not the Morrigan," she intoned. "And I did not allow it."

My breath shuddered from my lungs as I stared down into the inky water that had been such a brilliant, star-studded blue only moments before. I'd heard stories about this dragon mouth, but I'd always thought they were tall tales meant for fae children. A warning not to swim too deep into the dark. But those stories had been real. All of it was real. Faerie had once existed, and the fae had fled. Why? I swallowed hard. There was only one reason why, only one thing that made sense. If Caer wanted me to go through the portal to see it for myself, then I had been the cause. Me or Balor.

"You best go soon," Caer said, dropping back her head to stare up at the pure blue, cloudless sky. "Night is coming, and with it, comes a harsher darkness than you can even imagine."

She shoved me forward before I could answer. My feet stumbled beneath me, and I went flying into the lake, jeans and all. The water was cold and harsh as I slammed against it, limbs flailing as my mind caught up with what was going on. I thrashed in the lake, sputtering up water. "You could have given me a fucking warning."

"No." Her eyes flashed. "You would have found a way to back out of this. Now, go. Be the Morrigan you are."

Something about the tone of her voice edged me onwards, even though the logical part of my brain was urging me to swim to the bank, pull myself out of the lake, and run straight back to the car. I didn't have to do this. She might be the Goddess of Prophecy and Dreams, but I was the Morrigan. She couldn't force me to go through a long-forgotten portal into another world.

But I had to see it. The portal called to me. If

Faerie truly was real, I wanted to see it with my own two eyes.

With a deep breath, I dove downward. I'd never been the best swimmer. My heart was in the sky. But I swam all the same, heading deeper and deeper into the throbbing darkness that lay at the bottom of the lake. I peeled open my eyes, wincing as the water stung.

Nothing but darkness answered.

I dove on deeper. Further I went, swimming so far that I swore my lungs would burst.

Finally, when I thought my very last breath would abandon me, I spotted the hole. It was tiny, only big enough for a single person to squeeze through, if that. Branches snaked out of the sides of it, revealing a knotted, brambly path to the other side.

For a moment, I couldn't help but pause and stare. This was it. Faerie lay before me, and danger likely with it. I was all alone, with no warriors to back me up. I could turn back now, and no one but Caer would ever know. I could run from this. I could find another way to win, one that didn't lead into magical darkness.

But I didn't turn back. Instead, I swam on.

9

The portal through Faerie was both dark and light at the same time. Shadows pulsed along my skin like fingers of silken black. It whispered into my ears—or my soul—tempting me to forget myself, forget where I'd come from, and to give in to the pleasures that only the fae world could provide.

If legends were true, the fae used to entrap humans in their world, luring them from the safety of their human homes and into the savage, rollicking, pleasurable lands of magic, power, and destruction. Just as with the tales of the Lake of the Dragon Mouth, I'd never believed those stories to be true.

Now, I couldn't help but wonder, were all of mom's bedtime stories mere reflections of our true history? Were the fae the monsters of the past?

Maybe they were.

Maybe *we* were.

Despite the fact I'd lived most of my life outside of the system, I was very much a part of it now.

In the neverending darkness, a dim light shone

through the murky shadows. I reached out toward it, hoping against hopes that this portal would end.

It was the last thought I had before the shadows swallowed me whole.

~

I awoke on the bank of a lake much like the one Caer called home. Everything was the same. Sunshine, cloudless sky, an invisible breeze that ruffled my long, loose red hair and nothing more. I pushed up onto my elbows, glancing around. There was even a grass hut, roofless.

Still dizzy from my journey through the portal, I couldn't help but wonder if the lake had spat me right back out onto the bank, deeming me unworthy of a trip into the magical lands from whence the fae had come.

I stood and searched the cottage for Caer. There was nothing inside of it but dust and decay, the very corners of the floorboards curling up. Heart hammering hard, I returned to the edge of the lake, peering deep within its depths for a sign of what to do next.

There were no fish in these waters.

Caer had said this place had been destroyed. That was why the fae had fled. There was no sign of destruction here, but there was also no sign of life.

Of course, on the other side, the Lake of the Dragon Mouth seemed to exist in a world of its own. Maybe that was the case here, too.

I trudged up the hillside, stopping to check the rock where I'd left my jacket on the way down to the lake. It wasn't there. That final confirmation that I truly was no longer in the land of the humans made my heart speed up even more, so much so that it felt like it could launch a rocket into space.

Did they have an outer space here? Was there a London? Were there any cities at all?

At the top of the hill, I tried to steady myself on the solid trunk of a towering tree, sucking deep breath in through my nose. It smelled the same. There was oxygen to breathe into my lungs. I hadn't gone to another planet, even though it felt like I had. This was still Earth…only not really.

I pushed through the trees, sucking in the strangely fresh air. When I came to the edge of the tree line, I stumbled to a stop. Eyes wide, my hand flew to my heart as I gazed across the tumbling landscape of Faerie.

Ashen fields stretched out all around me. It was a sea of grey with no end in sight. Swallowing hard, I sat down hard on the small patch of grass that stopped suddenly, just before the magic of the Lake of the Dragon Mouth came to an end.

So, this was what Caer had meant. This was what had driven the fae out of their world. They'd had no other choice. As far as I could see, there was nothing left.

I closed my eyes, pulled my knees to my chest, and rested my chin on my jeans. No matter how long I stared, I couldn't drag my eyes away from the sight of all this darkness. Something terrible had happened here, more than just a war. More than warriors battling each other in the hope that another Queen or another King might take the crown.

This world had ended in a flash of bloody magic. How many fae had died from this destruction? How many lives had been lost?

And how much of this had been my fault?

Now that I was here, in Faerie, I would have access to those memories. All I had to do was call on them. I wanted to know the truth. I needed to know it. But the threat of what it might mean horrified me.

Could I ever look myself in the mirror again if the worst I feared was true?

Did the Morrigan—*did I*—destroy an entire world?

With a deep breath, I closed my eyes. I meant only to search through my ancient memories, but instead, sleep pulled me under, and my world was once again tipped upside down.

~

When I cracked open my eyes, the world of Faerie had been transformed. No longer did an ashen blanket cover every surface. Long stretches of brilliant green were spread out before me, violet, canary, and azure flowers peppered the expanse. I strode forward, eyes wide. A moment ago, Faerie had been gone, and yet here I was.

Two figures stood in the center of the field. They were backlit by a brilliant setting sun that caused streaks of vivid orange and red to skim along the horizon. Both figures were achingly familiar. One had flaming red hair that hung loosely down to an armoured waist. She held a spear in one hand and a sword in the other. Ravens circled her head, screaming bloody murder. She stood with her shoulders thrown back and her mouth open as she shouted words at her taller, broader companion.

Balor.

As I drew closer, distant shadowy shapes morphed into fully realised forms. In the background, on either side, two armies stood waiting for their ruler's command. My heart thundered hard as I understood exactly what I was witnessing. The Morrigan—*me*—facing off against her enemy. They were ready to go to war.

I began to run toward them, my feet sinking into the soft grass. I didn't know if this was some kind of vision or if I'd somehow been dropped into the past. Maybe I couldn't speak to them. But maybe I could. And maybe if I explained what happened when their fight came to a head, one of them would back down. To save Faerie.

But the world dropped out from beneath my feet. I fell, wind rushing up all around me. When my feet found purchase once again, I found myself in the dim, murky light within a castle's stone walls. A cool, damp whisper of wind ruffled the hair on my arms, making me shiver. Before me was a room, decorated in elaborate reds and golds. Flames flickered in the ancient fireplace. Fur rugs were spread out across the grey floor.

Once again, the Morrigan and the Smiter stood before me. This time, they embraced.

"Baleros," the Morrigan said in a sultry voice that sounded nothing like mine. I took a step closer, my heart in my throat. The Morrigan gazed up into Balor's twin orange eyes. There was no eyepatch.

There were no flames beaming out of his socket. This Balor—Baleros—was not even the smiter yet.

How curious.

"Morrigan," he said in such a familiar low growl that my body instinctively pulled me toward him. I forced myself to stop. If they somehow could see or hear me, I didn't want them to notice me now.

"Oh, how I have missed you. Why must you be a part of that horrid Court? Please, I beg of you. Join us. The Seelies are light. Step out of the shadowy darkness."

Baleros clenched his jaw and took a slow step back, extracting himself from the Morrigan's embrace. "You know I cannot do that. The Unseelie Court is my home."

My ears pricked up. Another myth, another legend come to life before me. I'd always thought the tales of the Seelies and the Unseelies were nothing more than fabled histories, much like the Greek Gods with their powers of the sun, the sea, and the dead. Based on legends, Faerie had once been divided into two Courts. The Seelie were the fae of light while the Unseelie were the fae of darkness. Neither were good nor evil. They were all fae with their own mischievous and wicked ways. But the two Courts had always been at odds, fighting for control of all the land.

My heartbeat pulsed a hectic beat. Was this where the battle had originated? Right here, in this room, by two fae on opposite sides of a neverending war?

"But *I* am Seelie," the Morrigan insisted, hurt flickering across her face. "You said that nothing would stop you from being with me. Not our Courts, not the war, nothing."

"And I meant it," he said in a growl, grabbing her chin fiercely in his hand. "I am going to make a deal with the crafter of magic, Credne, for a power that is unmatched by anyone else. All he wants in return is my vow to give him a position at Court. And it will help us end this war for good."

The Morrigan did not look impressed. She grabbed his hand and ripped it away from her skin. "If you love your Court and you mean to end this war, then you mean to destroy the Seelie Court. *My* Court. The one that my mother rules. The one that *I* will one day rule."

Even more interesting. When I'd thought of the Morrigan, I'd always imagined her fully-formed. But despite her varied, unending past, she had to come from somewhere. Once, she'd had a family. She'd grown up, just like any other fae. She'd had to come to grips with who she was and what she would do with her life. And here we were, at the very start of it all.

It made me want to sit down.

"Your mother is not fit to rule, and you know it. No one else knows about her pact with the shifters, but I do. They are our enemies. They want to steal our world. I've seen her go through the Lake of the Dragon Mouth to the mortal realm." A beat passed. "I know about her lover."

Fear flickered across the Morrigan's face.

"That's right," he said, taking another step toward her. "I know the truth about who you are. The truth about your shifter father. I won't tell a soul you're a mongrel. As long as you let me win."

The Morrigan slapped Baleros in the face.

10

I wanted to know more. So much more. My mind whirred with this new information. The original Morrigan, the very first, had been the product of a shifter and a fae. Just like me. As far as I was aware, this had never been the case before. All of the other Morrigans had been fully fae.

So, why me? Why now?

Before I could find any answers to my burning questions, the floor vanished beneath my feet once again. Soon, I was falling deep into that murky darkness. This time, I didn't scream.

When I landed on my feet, I was within that same room again. The light had changed. Sunbeams now stole across the stone floor, and the Morrigan stood at the window, staring out at the distance, a troubled expression on her face.

Baleros stood behind her. "I thought you would be happy about this. You want all of these battles to be over, don't you?"

"I do, but not like this." She whirled to face him,

eyes as fiery as his only visible one. A black eyepatch now covered the other. He must have taken the deal. Baleros had become the smiter now. "These are my friends, my family. I do not wish to see them die. I do not want to see them defeated."

He strode forward, took her hands in his, and dipped his forehead to meet her skin. He breathed her in deeply, his body shuddering as he captured her scent. "I can smell your fear. Do not worry. It will only be a small demonstration of my power. Only a few will get hurt, just enough to reveal the true depth of my power now. As soon as your Queen sees this, she will back down."

"And if she doesn't?" the Morrigan asked.

Baleros's expression darkened. "I will be forced to demonstrate a little more. But I may not need to, not if you speak to her first. Tell her how important it is to surrender."

The Morrigan was silent for a good long while before she finally nodded, tears staining her cheeks. "If it means this will all be over, I will speak to her."

Shocked, my eyes widened into saucers. This...this I hadn't expected. Baleros of the Unseelie Court, with darkness pouring through his veins, I could get. He wanted his Court to win. He wanted his fellow fae to survive. And he would do anything in his power to ensure they did. Sacrificing a few of his enemies was nothing.

But they were not the Morrigan's enemies. They were *her* fellow fae. I did not think she was capable of such a thing.

"Good." Baleros nodded. "And you will lure the warriors to the field?"

The Morrigan ground her teeth together, and then whispered, "I will."

~

Another fall. Another tumble through darkness. This time, I was back on the field. The two opposing armies stood ready and waiting while the Morrigan and Baleros argued in their armour.

This was it. The moment all of the other visions had been leading toward. The final showdown that caused the destruction of an entire world. How had Baleros gotten from the sacrifice of a few to the end of absolutely everyone?

"You tricked me," Baleros shouted into the Morrigan's face, his entire body brimming with intense, nervous energy. I could feel it even where I stood, between the bounds of whatever magic had brought me here. "You brought an entire army! Where are the dozen warriors you promised?"

"I was never going to bring you my subjects to be burned to a crisp. I was never going to sacrifice my own Court for your win. I'm protecting my fae just as you are protecting yours. And I will not apologise for that."

"So, you pick your shifter-loving Queen over an Unseelie rule? You pick her instead of me?" He shook his head, pain and anger whirling through his orange eye. "You said you loved me, Morrigan. You clearly do not know what love means."

"I know far more about love than you do, Baleros, with your smiting eye." She tightened her grip on her sword. "Hate, not love, is what has turned you against the shifters of the mortal realm. And it is hate, not love, that fuels your demand for Seelie deaths."

Baleros's mouth went wide. "*You* take the side of the shifters?" He barked out a harsh laugh. "I should have known. You are the daughter of one. Your heart is far too soft. They are wild, weak creatures who have no place in either realm. They are trying to infiltrate ours, to bring darkness to it with their ferocity. Your father has used your mother to get into Faerie, and he will die for it."

There was so much hatred in Baleros's voice. He sounded nothing like the Balor I knew. But the Morrigan sounded pretty foreign to me, too. Sure, she spoke of love, and she argued against hate, but there was nothing more than pure scorn whirling in her eyes. The Smiter and the Morrigan may have embraced before, but this was not a story of love. It was one of hate.

"You have sealed your fate," the Morrigan spit the words at Baleros's feet. "I thought I loved you, but I was wrong. You are a monster. You and every other Unseelie fae. And I will handle you like every monster deserves. You will die on this battlefield today, Baleros. And it will be by my own hand."

"Why wait?" Baleros grinned, the last remaining echoes of the male I knew and loved vanishing in an instant. He was replaced by someone else entirely. Someone cruel and wicked. Someone far more like Nemain than I could stand.

I didn't want to see any more of this. I wanted to leave, to go back to my own Balor and forget about everything that I'd seen here this day. But I didn't think I had a choice. The magic held my feet firmly in place. Even if I tried to walk away, I couldn't.

The Morrigan held up her sword, but Baleros shook his head. "No weapons. Just you and me and our powers. If you can defeat the fire that Credne has gifted to me, then you are far stronger than I thought. The strongest of us all. But you aren't."

With narrowed eyes, the Morrigan dropped one weapon to the ground, and then another. I wanted to yell at her to stop, to tell Baleros to keep his eye hidden beneath that black patch. But my mouth was as frozen as my feet were. I couldn't do a damn thing other than stand here and watch every single fae on this field die a fiery death.

The Morrigan bent her knees and curled her hands into fists while Baleros flipped up his patch. He kept his eye shut tight, his entire body trembling from the force of nature that was desperate to pour out. Morrigan opened her mouth, and a sound of terror filled my ears. It was the sound of battle, with a magic so fierce and strong that it shook me to my very core.

Streams of white hot magic shot out of her body just as Baleros opened his eye. Their magic collided: white hot light against orange flames. They pounded against each other, an unrelenting force that made the ground beneath my feet shake as if we were stuck inside the strongest earthquake the world had ever encountered.

The Morrigan shook. Baleros shook. Their bodies tipped toward each other just as the magic let out a shriek so loud my eardrums almost burst.

The magic shattered. It blew Baleros and the Morrigan halfway back across their fields. The storm of shifting magic tore into the air. It exploded into shards of flaming balls that crackled with white hot magic. They landed all around us, heavy bombs that shook the earth. The fire spread fast through the fields, far faster than any normal fire could.

On both sides of the battlefield, the warriors began to scream and run. Some were caught alight within seconds. Others ran with their limbs engulfed in magical flames. Others charged straight toward the Lake of the Dragon Mouth, fleeing from the terror behind them.

One ran past me, his eyes popping out of their sockets. He stopped just in front of me, glanced up, pointed, and then ran. My stomach flipped. Had he really seen me? Had I been here all this time?

I looked up. A flaming ball of magic was heading straight toward my head.

The world turned to dust.

~

It was a long time before I stood and made my way back through the forest, down to the Lake of the Dragon Mouth, and back through the portal to where the human world awaited me.

Caer was silent as I pushed up out of the lake, water trailing down my shivering body. She handed me a towel, which I took gratefully, even though the warming sun was already drying me fast.

"You saw," she said quietly.

I nodded, unable to answer out loud.

"The Morrigan and the Smiter both hold a similar type of power. It is volatile and dangerous. When weaved well, it creates the most wonderful things. The fae have never been more at peace than when the Morrigan and the Smiter have joined together to lead them."

Dread pooled in my veins at the silent *but* that followed.

"The worst destruction any world has ever seen has been when the two of you clashed. What you saw…it has never been that terrible since. Skirmishes, really, in comparison to the first war you ever waged against each other. Those skirmishes were nothing to fret over. You merely just destroyed each other, not the world."

I sunk down onto the grass and dug my fingers into the dirt, hating every word she spoke but knowing all of it was the truth.

"My prophecy is this: your bonds are ageless. You and he have always been linked. But yours will be the very last. And together, you will either save the world…or you will end it."

11

I cranked the heat to maximum, shivering against the buttery leather car seat. The cold had seeped deep into my bones on the trek back from the Lake of the Dragon Mouth, and the visions I'd seen in Faerie made that chill sink even deeper.

Caer's words echoed in my ears, so loud that I spun the volume dial of the radio all the way up to drown them out. Ever since I'd discovered that my bond with Balor sang of darkness and death just as much as it did of light, I'd been holding my breath in horrified anticipation of what might come next for the two of us. I'd known that things could get bad. I'd braced myself in case we lost our love to hate.

But this…this was something else entirely.

It was the destruction of an entire world.

And if we weren't able to keep a handle on the magic that throttled between us, it would end this one, too.

Hands shaking, I spun the steering wheel to the left to pull back onto the small country lane, but something heavy thudded onto the bonnet. A loud crash echoed through the car as I gripped the steering wheel tight in my hands, peering out the rain-soaked windscreen.

My heart thumped in time with the beat of the wiper blades. It was a body, one clad in all black. Blood oozed across the silver paint.

"Shit." I threw the gear into park and jumped out of the car, flipping my coat's hood over my head to block the rain. I ran between the twin beaming headlights and stared, trying to make sense of what had just happened.

It was a body, but it wasn't human.

From the thick, wiry fur that covered its face, I knew it was a shifter.

Blood roared in my ears as I stumbled back. This wasn't a coincidence.

It was some kind of trap.

"Hi, Clark," came a voice from behind me. I whirled in my rain-slick boots to find Aed's beefy form lurking silently in the downpour. He stood in the middle of the road, twin blades held in his thick hands.

For a moment, I thought he was alone. He'd come to fight me by himself.

But then, Elena stepped out from behind him, her face twisted up into a villainous grin. Her ever-present red cloak fluttered around her body, and it was as dry as the Sahara Dessert. "Hiya. Bet you didn't think you'd see me again."

Confusion rippled through me. The last time I'd seen this sorcerer, she'd been locked up tight in the dungeons of the Crimson Court. How had she gotten out? How the hell was she here now? With Aed? Had control of the Crimson Court been lost in the few hours since I'd left?

Someone must have helped this sorcerer escape.

Surely not. Nemain wasn't even in London. She was at the Ivory Court, trying to woo more fae to her murderous side.

"You may have the throne for now," Aed said, smiling at the confusion on my face, "but Nemain still has the bond. All she has to do is get to a few of your precious subjects, make a few orders, and they'll do whatever she commands."

My gut clenched tight. I didn't know how this had happened. Everyone had agreed to stay within the walls of the Court, to take no phone calls, just in case Nemain tried to get to them that way. As long as she couldn't make the order, they didn't have to follow her will. But somehow…she'd still managed to get to someone.

And if she could get to one, then how many others had been compromised?

"That's right." Aed grinned. "Someone has disobeyed you. Sucks, doesn't it? That's why the rulers of the Courts need their bonds. If you don't control the sheep, the sheep will control you."

I narrowed my eyes. "You do realise you're the sheep in this situation, right?"

"I willingly follow my Queen. Disobeying orders is the epitome of dishonour."

"You know what? I'm not going to disagree with you on that. But I've got a question for you. For following orders to be honourable, shouldn't there be a choice? If you blindly have to follow them, no matter what, then even the dishonourable of heart will obey. The choice has to be there to make it mean something."

Aed shifted in his boots and scowled. He tightened his hands around the blades and cast a glance toward Elena. "I know what you're trying to do, and it isn't going to work. You're trying to distract me from why I'm here. To kill you."

I arched a brow. "No longer following Nemain's orders, after all? Last time I saw you, you made it clear that she wants me taken alive, not dead. For the whole soul transfer thingy."

"Thanks to Elena here, Nemain has discovered a way to take your power when you're dead. It's no longer necessary for you to be alive."

Well, shit.

Aed continued. "Every fae under Nemain's command now has one order that supersedes them all. Kill the Morrigan."

I swallowed hard. This was a pretty shitty development and one I hadn't expected. Once again, it felt as if Nemain was operating on a larger chess board than any of us could see. Every time it felt like I was moving forward, she'd sweep in with a move that shook up every plan I'd concocted, knocking my pieces to the bloody ground.

A lone Fianna and a sorcerer were unlikely to take me down by themselves, but how many others had Nemain gotten to? Who at the Crimson Court had been given that order? Had Kyle? Had Elise?

Had Moira?

Pain shot through my heart at the thought of my

closest friends—my family—on a dedicated mission to end my life.

And yet, a part of me couldn't blame them, not after what I'd seen in Faerie. There were no good guys or bad guys in the deepest, darkest years of my past. The original Morrigan had been in the wrong, just as much as she'd been in the right. She had betrayed Baleros, and Baleros had betrayed her, too.

And now, we were both set on a path that would end the same. Maybe it would be better for the world if the Morrigan disappeared.

Gritting my teeth, I shook my head. I couldn't let myself go down that dark path. No doubt, Nemain would hope I'd hear this prophecy and think these very things. But I would not let history repeat itself. The Morrigan of back then hadn't known what the collide of powers would do to the world. If she had, she never would have used her power against Baleros. Right?

So, all I had to do was make sure I never found myself face-to-face with Balor on the battlefield. Easy enough.

"Stop stalling, Clark." Aed dragged his sword up into the air before him and smiled. "One might think you're scared to fight us."

"You wish." I snorted, though it was partially just for show. The battle before me was nowhere near as tough as many I'd already been through, but it was still two verses one. And I was the one.

I didn't just want to fly away this time. My bird could get me into the sky within seconds, leaving my attackers behind. But I needed to stand my ground.

Ideally, I would defeat Aed. He was a powerful

warrior and he'd been coming for me time and time again. He had no backup, other than the sorcerer. If there was ever a time for me to go up against him, it was now.

I needed to draw him into the forest first.

Slowly, I backed toward the tree line and disappeared beneath the canopy of thorny branches and big bulbous leaves. Aed rushed after me, the sorcerer by his side. His sword was raised high as he charged into the brush, coming at me without even the slightest hint of hesitation.

I arched my brow and gestured at the sorcerer. "You've been itching for a fight with me for months. You've finally got me alone now, but you brought someone else to do your dirty work for you. Too scared to take me on by yourself?"

Aed scowled. "I know your little tricks. Your spells you use to knock people out. She's here to counter whatever spell you throw at me. And she's here to stop you from flying away like the coward you are."

"Alright. How about this then? I won't use my magic," I said. "If you won't use the sorcerer's power either."

This was a risk. But it was the best way to get us on even ground. It only took seconds for the sorcerer's power to knock me unconscious. I couldn't afford for her to throw that spell at me while I was neck deep in the middle of a sword fight.

Aed considered my offer, and for a moment, I swore I saw respect flickering in his eyes. But that couldn't be right. Aed hated me. "You know what, Morrigan? You've got yourself a deal. We'll only use the weapons we have in our hands and nothing more. No magic. Just you and me and our swords."

"But…" Elena said, her thick eyebrows furrowing together.

"Go get in the car," Aed ordered. "You'll get to use your power some other time, but not tonight. This is between me and Clark."

The sorcerer frowned, but she didn't argue. After she disappeared through the trees, we heard a car door slam. With a smile, I raised my sword before me and bent my knees. Aed did the same, mimicking my fight stance.

My heart thundered in my ears as he rushed toward me. I lifted my weapon just in time, blocking him from slicing off my head. His powerful blow rang hard against my steel, and it knocked me several steps back.

I wet my lips and braced myself. Just in time to block another one of his attacks.

Before he could get another blow against me, I spun to the side and jumped out of his way. I lifted my sword and aimed it at his chest, but he was far too fast. He whirled and held up his sword, blocking my blow.

He took a step back then, dancing on his feet. And then he smiled. "You're better than I thought you'd be. Been practicing?"

"I have excellent teachers. Two of the best warriors I've ever met."

"Well, that's just not true, now is it?" he asked, still smiling. "Because you haven't been trained by me."

He rushed at me once again. This time, I wasn't ready. He'd distracted me with his words, caught me off-guard. His knife slid deep into my thigh, and blood spurted out of the open wound. I stumbled back, pain blazing through every inch of my body. Blood roared through my veins as my power screamed throughout all the centuries I'd lived.

Gritting my teeth, I held my ground as he charged once again. I clashed my steel against his, blocking his blow and then trying some of my own. But I couldn't do this. Not with gallons of blood pumping out of my thigh. My body was weak; sweat painted my face.

As he began to back away, I jogged toward a thick tree and scaled to the first branch. I needed a break. I needed a respite from this battle. My wound was aching, and blood continued to pour out of me. I could barely think straight, dizziness creeping in at the corners of my eyes. I knew that if I did not find somewhere to hide, then I would not make it through this fight.

Aed chuckled. He stared at me, a grin spreading across his devilish face. "You're running. You promised you wouldn't use your power. You gave me your word."

"I can run without using my powers." Taking a deep breath, I jumped from one limb to another, staying high in the trees. The only problem was, I could barely jump. Everything hurt. Darkness had begun to fill my vision.

I had to hurry, or else I'd die out here. Alone.

12

I couldn't go back to the Crimson Court, not until I was certain that every fae in that building wasn't out to kill me. Through the rain, I spotted an old pub with a single light outside. It was late, but the pub was open. A few cars squatted in the car park, signalling only a handful of patrons. That worked for me. The fewer humans who saw me bruised and bloody, the better.

Pushing the door open, I hobbled into the front lobby. My hair was plastered to my skin, and my teeth were chattering. An elderly woman with greying hair looked up from behind the bar and frowned. She motioned me closer, concern crinkling the corners of her eyes.

"You alright, love?" The neon lights of the bar blinked behind her.

Thankfully, she couldn't see the blood soaking into my jeans with all the rain that had darkened every inch of my clothes.

"My car broke down a few miles back, and I lost

my cell phone." My teeth chattered even harder. "I was hoping I could get a room here for the night and make a few phone calls to sort things out for tomorrow."

She nodded sagely. "Ah. An American. You lot aren't cut out for these winding country roads, now are you?"

I decided not to correct her and tell her I'd been living here for years. "Nope, and I'm not used to driving on the left side of the road either."

"That's all right, love." She disappeared through a door behind the bar, and then reappeared just beside me. The rest of the small pub had hushed as we'd spoken, and I could feel four pairs of curious eyes watching my every move. "We've got a room open. It's forty pounds for the night."

I grimaced. "My wallet is back in the car."

That part at least was the truth.

She was silent for a moment, and then gave a nod. "That's alright. You get settled on in and sort out your phone calls. In the morning, you can go collect your car and your wallet and pay me then."

"Really?" I gave her a genuine smile, shoulders relaxing. "That would seriously save me. Thank you."

She smiled and stuck out a hand. "Name's Sheila. You need anything, I'll be downstairs."

She left me alone in the squat little room that held nothing more than a standard bed and a tiny little table next to it. The place was big enough to turn around in, but not much else. Thankfully, I didn't plan to stay for very long.

Muffled voices caught my attention, and I edged over to a little vent in the floor, next to the window overlooking the street outside. Through the vents, I had an eerily clear view of the pub downstairs.

"What was all that about, Sheila?" A man, early forties, shaved head, and a beer gut, said from his stool beside the bar. "Giving out free rooms now, eh?"

Sheila bustled over to her station and refilled the man's pint. "Poor thing looked like she'd been drowned in the sea. Couldn't very well turn her away."

"She could be a con artist, you know." He drank a sip of his frothy beer.

"Nah." Another patron sidled up to the bar, this time a woman with hair as ginger as mine. "She didn't look the type."

The man snorted. "It's the ones that don't look the type that you have to watch out for."

Rolling my eyes, I pushed up from the floor. I didn't blame them for not trusting me. I'd rolled in out of the rain and asked to crash here for free. But that didn't mean I had to listen to it. Instead, it was time I made my phone call.

I dialled the main line of the command station, from memory. It was pretty much the only number I knew, due to the training I'd taken on when joining as a guard. After a few rings, Kyle answered.

"Crimson Court," he said, voice curious. We normally didn't get many phone calls on the main line.

"Yes, I would like to speak to Tiarnan or Ronan please, if either are around." Very formal, but I didn't want to be overly familiar just yet.

I didn't say who I was. I couldn't chance it. I also knew I couldn't stay on the line for long. Kyle was a master hacker and a whiz at anything tech-related. I didn't know if he could trace this call, but I'd worked as a private investigator long enough to know it was a possibility. The tracking software was out there. You just had to have access to it.

And Kyle probably had access to it.

"Clark? Where the hell are you? Shouldn't you be back by now? Balor has been looking for you." He cleared his throat and lowered his voice. "Nemain got to a few of the Crimson Court fae. You need to get back here."

I swallowed hard. God, I wanted to trust Kyle. He'd gone out on so many limbs for me, had trusted me when no one else had. But I couldn't. Because Nemain could have gotten to him, too.

"I'm aware. Can you pass me to Tiarnan or Ronan please? Or, better yet, can you give me one of their phone numbers?"

A long silence echoed through the phone. "Everything okay, Clark? You don't sound like yourself."

"Things will be fine once I speak to Tiarnan."

"Okay...Well, he's right here. I'll give him the phone."

"Just get his number, okay?"

Kyle sighed but did what I asked. As soon as I had the number, I hung up and dialled.

Tiarnan answered before the first ring even ended. "Clark, what the hell is going on? Why are you being all cloak and dagger?"

"Some of the House Beimnech fae have been compromised."

He snorted. "And now you sound like some kind of cop on a TV show. Yeah, we know that. It's been taken care of. There were three of them, and they're in the dungeons now. You need to get back here."

"I don't think that's a good idea."

A long beat passed. "What's going on, Clark?"

"I don't want to discuss this on the phone." Even though I was speaking to Tiarnan through his own private cell, I didn't put it past Kyle to find a way to listen in to every word I said. Tiarnan might even go along with it, if given a good reason. I needed to get off this call and fast. "Can you meet me somewhere? Tomorrow morning?"

"Clark, I've gotta admit, you're scaring me a little."

"Good." My voice was grave. "Meet me where we parked for our meeting with Caer. And don't tell anyone else. Not even Balor."

I gave him a time for our rendezvous and then hung up the phone, my heart hammering hard in my chest. Even though Tiarnan wasn't under Nemain's spell, I had no idea what I would encounter tomorrow. Would Tiarnan tell the others? Would my meeting with him turn into another trap?

The best thing for me to do would be to hide out here until I healed.

But there wasn't time for that.

~

The wound was festering when I checked on it in the morning. The whole area was swollen, red and yellow streaks spiralling out from the deep cut. Wincing, I pulled my now-dry jeans on over my shaking legs and stood for a moment in the middle of the room, trying my best to block out the pain.

Sheila, the owner of the pub, met me downstairs and drove me to my car. I had her park behind it, hoping she wouldn't notice the massive dead werewolf on the bonnet.

But the whole scene had been cleaned up. There was no wolf here this morning, and the blood had all been washed away. The only evidence that anything had happened was the large dent that cracked the paint.

Sheila popped up from behind me and startled me half to death. "The tow people coming soon, hon?"

I painted on a smile and cracked open my car door, fishing into the passenger seat for my wallet. "Yeah, they'll be here soon. Here's the money for the room. Thanks again."

She took the payment from me and smiled. "Need me to stick around in case they don't show up?"

"No, thanks." I grabbed my cell and held it up for her to see. "Looks like my phone was here all along."

"Alright, love. Well, you take care."

"Thanks, Shelia."

Thankfully, Sheila left me on the side of the road next to my "broken down" car, although I almost regretted my decision two seconds later when my ears filled with silence. Surely Aed wouldn't expect me to return to the scene of the crime only hours later, although he knew my car was here…so maybe he would.

Casting a quick glance around, I skulked past the tree line and hunkered down in a cluster of prickly bushes that would hide me from view if anyone came wandering down this quiet country lane. If Aed came for me, I would see him first.

Half an hour after our planned meeting time, I was two seconds away from ringing Tiarnan again, despite every warning bell clanging in my skull, when his car slid right up behind mine.

I waited with bated breath. The engine stopped. The car door opened. Tiarnan slid into view, cast a glance around, and then frowned as he leaned back against the bonnet of his car.

"You out here somewhere or do I need to call in the calvary?" he asked quietly.

"I'm here." I stood and pushed through the bushes, distinctly aware that I had several leaves and twigs stuck to the woolly jumper Sheila had lent to me.

His eyebrows knitted together. "Bloody hell, Clark." His gaze tripped down to my blazing leg. He sniffed the air, and his frowned deepened. "You're hurt. And you look like shit."

"Gee, thanks." I winced as I took another step toward him, and then stumbled. "I'm fine though. Really. Just had a little run-in with Aed and Elena. Someone let her out of the dungeons."

His expression darkened. "You're not okay. You can barely walk. We need to get you back to the Court, to the healers."

"No," I growled out the word.

Tiarnan's eyes widened. "It's your damn Court, Clark. You have to go back."

"It's mine in name. But it's Nemain's to command. You know, probably better than I do, that she can command every single one of them to do anything she damn well pleases. All she has to do is whisper the words in their ears. We tried to stop that from happening, but it's already started. And from here, it'll spread. If it hasn't spread already."

Tiarnan crossed his arms over his chest. "That hasn't stopped you before. You always knew that was a risk."

"That was before I knew what the newest order was." I winced again as I took another step and levelled my gaze at Tiarnan. "She's ordered every single fae under her command to kill me on sight. If I step foot back inside the Crimson Court, an entire mob of fae who I've sworn to protect might very well rush to kill me."

His expression darkened, and he let out a low whistle. "Damn. I thought she wanted you alive."

"She doesn't any longer."

"You're strong, Clark. You have a good chance of holding your own against that kind of attack."

"No, I don't." I closed my eyes. "What do you think would happen if Kyle, Elise, and Moira tried to murder me? That I'd kill them in order to protect myself? That I'd shove a blade into their hearts?"

A beat passed as sadness filled his eyes. "No, I don't suppose you would."

"I want to go back to the Court more than anything. But I can't."

"What are you going to do then? Give up the throne?"

"Never," I said, wobbling as a new wave of pain went through me. "I'm going to the Ivory Court, and I'm going to take on Nemain."

But before I could explain my plan, consciousness left me.

13

I woke with a start, certain that I was two seconds away from death. My fist flew up before me, and I kicked out a leg. It made contact, and a muffled *oof* answered the blow.

"Careful, tiny bird. You've been through a lot, but the wolf won't take a kick to the balls without retaliating."

I sat up fast and glanced around to find myself on Ronan's ratty sofa, his cage hunkering in the back corner of his warehouse. "Wait. Where the hell am I?"

He pursed his lips, frowned. "Did Aed hit you in the head, too? You've been here a shed load of times."

"No, I mean, *why* am I here?" I glanced around. "And where's Tiarnan?"

"Tiarnan brought you back here after you collapsed from that nasty gash in your thigh. Your body started shifting from bird form back to fae form, over and over again, without your control. Trying to heal itself, I imagine. Tiarnan didn't know what to do for you, so he brought you here."

"I shouldn't be here." I jumped to my feet and winced. Even though I'd shifted and somewhat healed, my thigh still felt raw. "Everyone knows about our connection. This is one of the first places they'll look."

"Ah. You're still on about Nemain's orders."

I glared at him. "Yes, I'm still *on about them*. Every fae in London is after my head."

"You're safe here," he drawled, crossing his arms and leaning lazily against the wall. "This place is loads more secure than you'd expect, and I won't let anyone in."

As if to answer his statement, a loud boom shook the door to his warehouse. We were both on our feet in an instant. Ronan frowned and strode to the back of the room, peering down at some monitors at a computer station he must have set up since I'd lived here.

"Well, look what we have here. Our first set of visitors." He tried to make his words sound lighthearted, but a wave of nausea drew all the blood from my face.

"Believe me now?" I asked in a snap.

He ran a hand down his face before yanking open one of his desk drawers. He pulled out a handgun and cocked it. "I never said I didn't believe you. Just that you'd be safe here."

But I barely heard his words, my eyes too focused on the weapon in his hands. "What's the gun for?"

"What do you think?"

"You can't shoot them." Eyes narrowed, I stumbled toward him. I didn't know what I planned to do. Wrestle him for the gun? At the moment, he could just hold it up above his head, and I'd never get ahold of it. I hated being weak. I didn't want to be taken care of. I hadn't felt so hopeless in such a long time.

Added to that, it had been two days since I'd seen Balor, and the hours seemed to stretch out into endless eternity. The bond between us still pulsed with magic. I felt more drawn to him than I ever had before. But Caer's warnings rang in my ears, and my mind was still filled with the visions I'd experienced in Faerie. No matter how much I wanted him, no matter how much my heart longed for his, I couldn't let our love destroy another world.

"I've got your sword." He pointed at the corner wall where my sword sat waiting for me, and then he grabbed another gun from his drawer. "There's a hidden back exit. They're focused on the front. This is our chance to get out of here."

My heart thumped hard. "I thought you just said this place is secure."

"Sure." He shrugged. "If one fae came. Or two. But there are about twenty out there, and they've got a sorcerer to back them up."

"Twenty?" Eyes wide, I rushed over to the monitor to search for any familiar faces. Moira, Kyle, Elise. I let out a shaky breath of relief when there wasn't. It was just the Fianna and several fae I didn't recognise —probably from House Beimnech.

"Come on," Ronan said. "Let's go. I'll give Tiarnan a ring and see if he has any suggestion on where you should go."

Just like me, Tiarnan had spent some time on the run. We needed somewhere off the beaten track, somewhere none of us had ever spent before. Something connected to no one and nothing that anyone could trace. Problem was, Kyle would know a lot of my tricks. He'd worked with me long enough to know how I thought. If anyone could track me down, it would be him. So, I'd have to think like Nemain. I'd have to be five steps ahead of everyone else.

At least Ronan wasn't going to try to convince me to return to the Court after this. Silver lining?

After Ronan made the call, I grabbed my weapon, and we headed to the door. Tiarnan was waiting for us outside, but he wasn't alone. He'd brought Balor with him. A heavy sense of betrayal washed over me, and I shot the harshest of glares at the fae I had trusted. He merely lifted his hands to his sides and shrugged.

"He was losing his bloody mind," Tiarnan said by way of an explanation. "I figured he's not under Nemain's spell. It's okay for him to know what's going on."

I hadn't told Tiarnan about my little trip into Faerie or the prophecy I'd learned from Caer. At the time, I hadn't been ready to speak it out loud. Maybe if no one ever knew, maybe if I avoided Balor for the rest of my life, no one would ever have to find out what we would end up doing to the world.

Ashes. Death. Decay.

"Clark." Balor threw his arms around me and pulled me close, crushing me to his chest. His smell consumed me, that intoxicating mixture of leather and gin. My entire body stiffened, even as it yearned to give into his embrace, to curl up inside of him and never face the world again.

I could get lost in this. We could run away. If we weren't part of the fae world, then we'd never have to face the consequences.

ALL'S FAE IN LOVE AND WAR

Ashes. Death. Decay.

I pulled out of his grip and stepped back, casting my eyes to the ground. "I know you're probably upset with me for ghosting you the past two days, but let's do our best to stay calm."

A beat passed before he spoke. When he did, his voice sounded pained. "Because of our bond. Because of our magic. That's why you've been avoiding me, why you've been turning to everyone else. Even when you're hurt."

"Please," I said, whispering. "The last time we saw each other, we shattered a window. Now, I'm on the run for my life. Our bond is volatile. Let's not provoke it."

"Tiarnan told me," he said in a low growl that made me shiver. "Nemain has given the order for your death. Come back to the Court. You're safe there. She only got to a handful of fae, and we've identified every last one of them. They're in the dungeons. They cannot get to you."

I flicked my eyes up from the ground to gaze into his piercing eye. And then I glanced at his patch. Beneath it had once been the eye that had burned an entire world. That eye was gone now. Nemain had destroyed it. My heart lifted at the thought. Did that mean the prophecy was wrong?

"I can't risk that," I said, instead of voicing all my thoughts out loud. "We don't know exactly who she got to in the Court. She would have ordered them not to share that kind of information with you or anyone else. Hell, Moira and Elise could be parroting whatever she says." Balor's face clouded over. "You know it's true."

"Dammit," he muttered, turning toward Tiarnan. "What do you think we should do here?"

It was the first time I'd ever seen him turn to the ex-Fianna for advice. Once upon a time, they'd hated each other. Now, they were working together, even to trap me into a confrontation with my mate.

And maybe it was yet another sign. The Balor—or Baleros as he'd called himself then—was far more vicious, far more feral than the male who stood before me now. He'd been wicked, deep down inside of his heart. The Balor I knew had only ever been wicked for show, to fool the world into thinking he was hard. Beneath it all, he loved the fae so deeply that he'd sacrifice anything, including his own life.

"Fionn always kept safe houses hidden from the knowledge of anyone, including his closest advisors and his most trusted warriors. I assume you have something like that, too?"

Balor gave a slow nod. "He learned that trick from me."

"Take her there, at least until we've worked out how deep Nemain's orders go."

"That won't look good," Balor argued. "The ruler of the Crimson Court hiding away from her own people."

"No one but us has to know why she's gone," Tiarnan said. "Besides, it's better for everyone if we don't start a war from within. If Clark steps foot inside the Court and dozens of fae swarm in with the kill...I fear there's no coming back from that."

Balor sighed and dragged a hand down his face. "It's a good plan, even if it isn't ideal." He turned to me. "Clark?"

I nibbled on my bottom lip. A safe house hidden in London could work if I had any desire to stay in London. But I knew Balor would try to stop me if he knew I planned to go after Nemain in the Ivory Court. I didn't want to lie to him. I'd sworn I never would. But that was before I found out our love could destroy the world.

"I'll go to the safe house," I said.

14

*B*alor escorted me to the safe house himself, even when I tried, half-heartedly, to argue otherwise. I didn't want to risk another confrontation with him, even over something as simple as this. One wrong word, and our shared magic could blow a hole in the concrete. I'd rather not.

So, I went along, compliantly.

"You're quiet," he grunted as he slid his car to a stop on a long, hushed street in Chelsea. The houses sat in rows, tall and luxurious, with their red brick facade and white trim. Trees were spaced out in even increments, and potted plants sat beside the wrought-iron railings that led up to colourful doors.

"And agreeable," he added when I didn't respond. "That's not like you. Aed must have really shaken you up."

It wasn't Aed who had left me shaken.

"It's been a long day," I said. "And a long night before that."

He pushed out of the car, strode to my side, and

cracked open the door. Such a gentlemanly move. Surely not the kind of gesture a male would make if he couldn't control the fiery power inside of him.

I climbed out of the car and gave him a tight smile of thanks.

Balor led me into the building. The safe house was on the top floor, three small rooms that were bigger than any flat or apartment I'd ever held on my own. The place had been furnished nicely. In the living room, two comfortable sofas set in an L-shape facing a widescreen TV. A bookcase held a collection of tomes on the history of the fae world and several pieces of fiction that had been published by members of the Court.

There was a small bedroom with a king-sized bed squashed into the corner, looking out on the streets below. The kitchen was fully stocked. The refrigerator was full of fresh meat and vegetables, and a fruit bowl held apples, oranges, and bananas that must've been picked up only hours ago.

This might be somewhere that fae only went when fleeing from danger, but it felt like a home away from home to me.

"This looks great, Balor. Thanks." I sunk into the sofa and leaned back, closing my eyes. The only thing it was missing was a gin bar.

"I suppose you don't wish for me to stay."

"Balor." I sighed. "You know I do."

The cushion beneath me shifted as he took his place by my side. A warm, strong hand curled around mine. Even that smallest of gestures made me shudder. It was impossible to resist him, even knowing what had happened all those centuries ago in Faerie.

"You haven't said a word about Caer," he said quietly. "I take it she said some things that didn't sit right with you."

Understatement of the century.

I opened my eyes, shifted on the sofa to face him, and stared deep into his orange-red eye. Reaching out, I pressed the tip of one finger against his patch. "You know, you don't need to wear this anymore."

"Yes, I do," he said simply.

I puffed out a breath. "No, you don't. I know you think it will reveal some sort of weakness, but it won't. Hell, I think it'll do the opposite. It's a war story. A scar. Evidence of who you are and what you've been through. A demonstration of your courage. You say that leaders should never hide. So, don't hide this."

He let out a heavy sigh and shifted slightly away, his muscles rippling as his body went tense. "Clark, hiding this is the best thing I can do for everyone."

"It doesn't make a difference, Balor," I insisted, tightening my hand around his. "I've seen it. It doesn't make you look weak at all. It makes you look strong."

"You have not seen it," he said quietly. "Because if you had, you would be burnt to a crisp."

My heart thudded against my ribcage, and the entire world went suddenly still around me. "What are you talking about? Your eye is gone. Nemain destroyed it."

"There's something I haven't told you, Clark. I kept meaning to find the right time, the right moment. But that moment has never come. So, I suppose now is as good a time as any." He turned to face me again, his single red eye flickering with power. "I made a deal with Credne. And I got my eye back."

I sucked a sharp breath in through my nose and sat back. "You did what?!"

"When you went north with Tiarnan and Ronan to scope out House Futrail, I sought out Credne. He gave me back the power of my eye. I've been keeping it a secret because I don't want Nemain to find out. When we finally come to blows with her again, she won't be expecting my flames. With your power and my restored eye combined, there is no chance that she can beat us."

Thunder roared in my ears as I stared at the fae who sat before me. I'd convinced myself that the absence of his eye meant something, that the world would be safe, that nothing would burn.

But it was back.

I stood quickly from the sofa and strode to the window. Tears filled my eyes. "You said you made a deal. What was your end of the bargain?"

"You don't seem pleased." He stood and frowned.

"What was your part of the deal, Balor?"

"I only vowed to give him a position at Court."

A position at court. That was exactly what the original Balor had promised the magic crafter, Credne. How could this be happening? How could so many things happening now reflect what had happened in the past? The parallels were too much to ignore. It made everything seem inevitable.

Everything inside of me hurt. My heart, my stomach, even the blood in my veins. Balor had made a deal for his eye. The very same deal that had gotten him that power in the first place. History was repeating itself. If we kept moving down this path...there was only one way this all would end.

"I'm very tired," I said, breathless. "Would you mind if I went to bed?"

His frown deepened. "What is wrong, Clark? I don't understand why you would be upset by this? The deal hardly matters. It's meaningless. And it means we have an advantage that Nemain will never expect. This is a *good* thing, Clark. Can't you see that?"

"Of course I see that," I said in a tight voice. "But I really do need some rest. Despite all my Morrigan powers, I'm not like you. I can't keep going on, like a fully-charged battery. I'm still recovering from Aed's attack, after all. My thigh hurts."

At least that was the truth.

"Is this because you're worried I'll try to take back the throne, now that my power has returned to me?"

I whipped toward him, hand on my chest. "How could you even think something like that?"

He stalked closer to me, frowning. "I wouldn't have thought it at all, but nothing about your reaction makes sense to me, Clark. I thought you'd be happy I got my power back. Instead, you look scared."

The shadows were pulsing around us again. I needed to put a stop to this conversation. Now. Before things got worse. This was getting far too close to what I'd seen in the past. Two fae at odds, fighting over power.

"I look scared because I feel scared." I turned to face him, bracing myself for the words I would have to say to him. "The magic of our bond terrifies me. It's scarier than anything I've ever encountered in my life, and that includes fighting against all of my enemies. The vamps. The wolves. The Sluagh. Because it's fighting with you."

He frowned. "But it's not fighting with me, Clark."

"It's close enough." I sucked in a deep breath, tear stinging my eyes. Everything within me wanted to reach out and press my hands to his chest, to breathe him in. I wanted him close to me. I never wanted to leave his side. But I didn't know how we were going to deal with this. I'd only just found out about the past. How could I think about our future with those images echoing inside my mind?

"What are you trying to say?" he asked, his voice and his face bleeding with pain.

"I don't know, Balor." I curled my hands into fists. They shook by my thighs. "Everything between us has been so hard. Maybe we were never meant to be anything more than what we are."

"And what *are* we, Clark? Because I was under the impression that we were a hell of a lot."

My eyelids fluttered shut. "I don't even know how to explain it."

"I'll tell you what we are," he said. "We're mates. We're lovers. We are two sides of the same coin, soulmates who have somehow found each other after decades lost. I don't understand what is happening between us, but we will figure it out. We always do."

Pain lanced through my heart. "Maybe you're right. Maybe nothing bad will come of the violent magic that charges between us every time we're together. But right now, I need some time. Right now, I'm far too exhausted to fight against you or that power."

Pain flickered across Balor's face and everything inside of me hurt. The last thing I wanted to do was cause him pain. Hell, it was hurting me, too.

But I also wasn't lying. I did need time. Time to process how I felt about the Faerie revelations, time to figure out if there was a way for us to survive our bond.

Until I did, I couldn't see the male I loved.

15

The news about Balor's powers made me rethink my plans. More than ever, I wanted to take down Nemain and get this whole thing over with before our bond became too much for either of us to handle. It was all tied back in to my ancient enemy. This war. This fight. The future of Faerie. If we got through this, we would come out alright in the end.

But we couldn't get through this if we played right into Nemain's hands.

The next morning, I gave Ronan a call and waited on the front stoop of the Chelsea brownstone for him to arrive. In the end, I hadn't left the safe house, even with the threat of my clash with Balor hanging over my head. I'd seen the look on his face. He would not come back here after our fight, at least not for a few days.

"Pretty nice digs you got here," Ronan said in a low whistle as his eyes scanned the street. A steel grey haze covered everything as the morning sun edged into a winter sky, but it was still enough to highlight the oozing money of this place. "But I thought you weren't allowed to tell anyone where you are."

"I'm allowed to do whatever I damn well please," I snapped.

"Okay, okay." He held up his hands with a laugh. "No need to get your cob on. You and Balor have a fight or something?"

"That's a long and complicated story that I can't really go into right now." I sighed and kicked at the stone step. "Balor got his flaming eyeball back."

Ronan's brows winged upward. "You serious?"

"As serious as a flaming eyeball."

"Shiiiiit." He sunk down onto the step beside me, dragging a hand down his face. "That's good, right? That'll give us some serious firepower—pun intended—during the battle against Nemain."

"Sure. Or we could try to prevent that from even happening."

A sly grin spread across his face. "I'm listening."

"She likes to set traps for us, right? How many times has she made us think we were doing one thing when we were really following her script down to every last damn line?"

"Thanks to her power. She's good at anticipating our moves."

"Which is why we should do something totally unpredictable. If she's good at knowing what people will do, maybe she already knows about Balor's eye. If she does, she'll have a contingency in place. She'll be ready for it."

He gave a slow nod, eyebrows furrowing. "It makes sense. But how do you know that she won't be anticipating this trap?"

"Because my original plan, and what I really want to do, is to go after her. I feel it in my bones, Ronan. I want to track her down at the Ivory Court and end this once and for all." I flicked my gaze toward him and saw understanding. "She will know I want to go to her and kill her. So, she'll be expecting it. Staying here in London goes against every single urge I have deep within my bones."

"So, you're going to do what you *don't* want to do, in order to throw her off the scent?"

"Exactly," I said with a nod. "Setting a trap feels like playing the game her way. It also means lying to some people, which I don't like to do. But if it means we might end this entire thing before it becomes an all-out war..."

"It's worth it." He nodded, closed his eyes, pain flickering across his face. He'd seen so much blood in his life. I knew he didn't want to see any more of it. "Whatever it is, I'm in."

"Good." I gave him a strained smile. "Because I'm going to need you to go tell some fibs. I'd do it myself, but..."

"You need to stay away from Court."

"I mean, they've all got an order to kill me." I grimaced. "So, here's what we're going to do."

JENNA WOLFHART

"Clark?" Elise's eyes widened when she strode into Gordon's Wine Bar, her silver hair glistening even beneath the dim lighting. She rushed over to me, looked me up and down, and gave me a light tap on the arm. I think it was supposed to be a punch, but she was far too kind for that. "Where the hell have you disappeared to and why didn't you tell me anything? What's going on? Why are you here? I thought I was meeting with Ronan."

"I need to read your mind." I braced my arms on the table and searched her eyes for a reaction.

She stiffened. "What? Why?"

"I can't tell you," I said, passing her a drink. Gin and tonic, to take the edge off. No one liked being read, not even my closest friends. "But it's important."

Her eyes slightly widened. "This has something to do with Nemain, doesn't it? You know I'd never follow her orders."

"Not voluntarily," I said quietly. "Listen Elise, I'm sorry to have to be this way, but I either need to read your mind or I need to go. I'll explain after, but right now, that's all I can say."

A beat passed where one of my nearest and dearest friends could only stare at me. I knew she might be hurt, but I couldn't risk telling her anything she could feed back to Nemain, not until I was certain that her mind hadn't been fiddled with.

"Okay," she said, pressing her lips into a thin white line. "I'll agree to this, as you're my Queen. But I have to be honest, Clark, as a friend, I'm hurt."

My heart squeezed tight.

The last thing I wanted to do was upset Elise. She

wouldn't hurt a fly, even if that fly had fangs. She knew just as well as I did that Nemain could have gotten to her easily enough and twisted her mind against me.

I tried not to draw things out. Getting it over quickly meant she didn't have to spend long with someone digging around inside of her thoughts. I dove in without any preamble, reading everything she saw, heard, felt, and knew from the past few days.

Nothing in her mind suggested that she was being controlled by Nemain. She was scared, sure, and she was a little bit annoyed. But she was Elise.

Quickly, I filled her in on everything that had happened, leaving out the details relating to the bond I had with Balor. Eventually, I would tell everyone about the prophecy, but Balor needed to hear it from me first.

"I knew she was trying to get to fae inside of the Court, but I had no idea she was ordering everyone to kill you." She scrunched up her face. "This could get really bad really fast."

"That's why we need to get this over with before it does get bad really fast. We're going to set a trap for Nemain. And I need your help."

She nodded eagerly. "You know I'll do anything. Just say the word."

"I'm going to need two things from you." I smiled, glad that we were back on the familiar ground of plotting against our enemies. "First I'm going to need you to leak some information to her warriors. Aed is still out there, running around trying to kill me. He needs to hear that I've given up the throne. He'll pass the information on to Nemain, and she'll come running."

Elise cocked her head. "Do we really want Nemain to come running? She'd just be running straight into a court who is bound to listen to her every word."

"That's why we're going to trap her," I said, closing my eyes for a moment. The last thing I wanted to be doing was plotting someone's death. Killing wasn't the answer in most cases. But I didn't see any other way to get around this one. If the fae of the Crimson Court were going to live their lives without her presence bearing down on them, she either had to pass her power on to someone else or she had to die.

And Nemain never handed over power willingly.

Elise pursed her lips. "But what about the bond? You won't have anyone to fight by your side, not without her commanding them herself. Or do you really plan to take her on alone, Clark?"

"That's why I'll have Ronan and Tiarnan there to back me up as warriors." I paused for a moment, letting my words sink in, and then I continued on with my plan. "I'm also going to need you to put a glamour on me. One that no one will recognize, not even Balor."

"Glamour." A little smile tickled Elise's lips. "I like it. Who do you want to be?"

"Someone who looks nothing like me. Short hair, bleach blonde, maybe kind of tall?"

Elise laughed. "You know you can't change your height in a glamour."

"Dammit." I grinned back. "You can't fault me for trying."

Elise continued to laugh, but then her smile died from her lips. Her expression went somber, serious.

"Are you sure this is a good idea? It sounds like you've thought it through, but you never know what Nemain has planned."

"To be honest, I have no idea if this is the right move or not." I placed my hands flat on the table and took in a deep breath for courage. "But we can't sit back anymore. It's time to make our move."

16

The trap was set. Tiarnan, Ronan, Elise, and I had managed to set a chain of events in motion that would draw—hopefully—Nemain back to London and play right into our hands. All we had to do now was wait. As my new, secret identity that Elise had gifted me, I decided I'd wait things out by checking up on the Court. All I had to do was avoid running into Balor. He would sniff out my scent in a heartbeat, but no one else would be able to tell who I was.

Rolling back my shoulders, I pressed down my bright pink shirt and strode through the front doors of the Crimson Court. I stopped for a moment in the glistening lobby, taking in the bright chandelier that hung glowingly overhead. I breathed in the scent. Magic, salt, and smoke. An intoxicating combination that made me never want to walk out of this place.

It felt like home.

In the distance, I heard a familiar voice. Balor was down the hallway, and he was coming closer. Despite the tiny voice in the back of my head urging me on, I couldn't help but want to see his face.

And then another voice drifted toward me. One I vaguely recognised. A female. The bond between us snapped tight, and jealousy slithered through my veins like poison.

Frowning, I pressed my back against the wall and listened in.

"I worry about Clark's intentions here. I know she is the reincarnated version of the Morrigan, or so she says, but that does not give her immediate access to the throne," the voice said.

Balor let out a growl of disapproval. "When the Morrigan was last alive, she was Queen of Faerie."

"But Faerie isn't even really a thing anymore," the voice said. "Times have changed. We no longer live in the Middle Ages. Faerie has split up. We're seven Courts now, with our own rulers, born into royalty. Clark was born by a no-name American fae and a shifter. How does that give her the right to rule the European fae?"

My heart hammered hard, and my mouth went dry. I didn't know who this fae was, but her words cut deep. They were also not wrong. Once, the Morrigan had meant everything to the fae. She had been a fearless leader who had led them with power, strength, and wisdom. I'd always found it hard to believe that it was me, because I had none of those qualities. Sure, I could wield some impressive power, often accidentally, but I wasn't the intimidating presence she'd always been. I was just stubborn as hell.

And the fae had moved on from her reign, just like this stranger had said.

Should I just walk away from this? Should I give up the right to rule? Did I even have that right to begin with? Maybe if I let go of this entire thing, maybe if I stepped down, the way the original Morrigan hadn't, then my clash with Balor would never happen.

Maybe by giving up the throne, I would save the world.

"I know you have your doubts about Nemain's abilities, and you hold a grudge against her because of what happened to your sister, but she has knowledge of the fae and experience the Morrigan will never have."

Ah, and there it was. The reminder of why I was fighting so hard to win. Nemain. If I stepped aside, she would have fewer obstacles to block her ascent to the throne of Faerie. And there was no telling what kind of world this realm would become if she had that kind of power to wield.

"You speak as though Clark does not possess the full knowledge of all the Morrigans. And the Morrigan is much older and stronger than Nemain."

"If she possessed the full knowledge, she would not behave like a bumbling baby fae in way over her head." The female laughed. "Every single time, she plays straight into Nemain's hands."

My spine stiffened. Okay, I'd had enough now. Who the hell was this fae?

Holding my breath, I craned my head around the corner to peer into the corridor where they'd stopped for their chat. I had to hold back a gasp of surprise when I saw who it was. Lizzie, the fae from House

Futrail who had helped me escape from the dungeons there.

Why was she no longer being confined? What had she said to get free?

And why was she no longer trying to fight back to get to her home? Dread pooled in my gut. Whatever was happening here, it wasn't good.

She strode seductively toward Balor, and a smile curled on her lips. "I know you're mated to her, but surely you desire someone more your size. A full fae, perhaps, who can withstand all your power, who gratefully accepts it."

My hands curled into shaking fists by my sides, and I had to force myself to push away from the wall. What was going on here? And how could I handle this without losing control of my power? If I stormed in there now, I knew what would happen. Balor would be angry I'd eavesdropped, and Nemain's lackey would get exactly what she wanted: more strife between us.

No, I needed to do something else.

Biting my tongue, I slid my cell out of my back pocket and fired off a text to Elise.

Invent some kind of emergency to get Balor to the command station.

A moment later, Balor's cell rang. He answered, a frown deepened the lines around his eyes, and then he bid his farewell to the asshole of a fae named Lizzie. He strode off down the corridor, and I couldn't help but notice how keenly she watched him go. Jealousy was still hot lava in my veins. I didn't know how much of her flirtation was an act and how much of it was real, but goddamn, I did not like it.

I waited until she'd turned away before I drifted

into the corridor like a little lost puppy in need of a pat on the head.

"Oh, hi," I said with a smile, placing a hand on her arm, just to see how she'd react to my touch. "You must be new here. I'm Norah."

She brushed my hand off her arm and smiled absently. "Excuse me, Norah. I was just in the middle of something."

"Ah." I smiled knowingly. "Balor, huh? Careful with that one."

She cocked her head, suddenly far more interested. "And why is that?"

"You really *are* new." I arched a brow. "Now that he is no longer my Prince, I can speak freely. Balor is...well, he's a fuckboy. He goes from female to female and discards them like old sweet wrappers. For a blink, we thought he might finally have found himself a wifey, but he's thrown her out with the trash now, too."

Her eyes went sharper. "You mean Clark?"

I mock widened my eyes and cast my gaze to the ground, taking a step back. "I've said too much."

Her hand landed on my arm, and her grip went steel tight. Her voice was harsh, and her teeth ground together when she spoke. "Tell me more. Are the two of them finished? Is that why she's not here?"

I nodded my head, eyes so wide I swore the sockets might pop. "The Morrigan abandoned us and her crown."

I dove into her head.

I wish I didn't have to do this. I don't want to go against Clark, and I hate trying to turn everyone here against her. But I have no other choice. Nemain got to one of the fae in here, and she got new orders to me. If only I could warn Clark...

For a moment, it seemed as though Lizzie stared right into the very core of my soul. There was so much rage that flashed in her eyes. She was looking at the board, trying to move the chess pieces in a way that only Nemain could do.

She let go of my arm. "I'm afraid that I need to be by myself to process this information. Nice meeting you, Norah."

And with that, she scurried down the corridor and out of sight. I let go of the breath I'd been holding and sagged against the wall. There. That should do it, if Nemain wasn't already on her way. She thought Clark Cavanaugh had flown into the wind after fighting with Balor. A Balor who no longer had a flaming eye.

In her mind, there would be nothing standing in her way. She would come for the throne. Her ambition would have it no other way.

17

The throne room was quiet and empty. It always was, save for special occasions. It was a relic of a time that had long been forgotten. The fae kept their traditions, but for the most part, they had moved on with the times, just like the humans had.

Even after leaving Faerie, my memories of that time had continued to flood my mind. It was as if the floodgates had been opened, and I would never be able to close that door again. The fae were the ones who had developed the system of the Courts, of royalty, of kings and queens. When they had fled the burning lands of Faerie, they had brought the Courts along with them. Humans had then adopted them for themselves.

I approached the pile of crimson skulls and dragged my hand along the bones, stopping to smile at the cauldron I'd bought for Balor all those weeks ago. Back when things between us seemed hard, but they were the easiest they'd ever been. Back when the only worry was if I'd accidentally fall into his bed.

I yearned to go back to that, but I doubted we ever could.

"I knew you were here." His voice boomed against the cavernous walls. A slip of fear went down my spine, and I kept my focus on the throne before me instead of what lay behind: Balor.

I didn't even pretend to be Norah. He knew it was me. "Who told you? Lizzie?"

"So, that is why she is acting strangely," he replied.

I whirled to face him, heartbeat tripping. "Why is she no longer tied up? You realise she's working for Nemain, don't you? Otherwise, the bond would still be forcing her to get the hell out of this building."

"You think I'm a fool, even after everything we've been through together," he said, voice hard.

And there it was. The clash. The conflict. We couldn't even speak for two minutes without turning our anger on one another.

"I don't think you're a fool. I do question why you'd let her walk around whispering bullshit into your ear."

His gaze darkened. "You were eavesdropping on our conversation."

"And?" I asked, brow arched. "This is my Court. I can do as I damn well please."

Whoops. I shouldn't have said that. I was trying so hard to keep things calm between me and Balor. The last thing I wanted was to stir up the magic, those deep shadows that sparked between us. Shadows that we brought into the world ourselves. Deep down, I knew what they were. A relic of the clash between our powers from so many centuries ago. It had been with us all these years.

"That may be so, Clark," he said, nostrils flaring. "But I am your mate."

Memories flashed through my mind. That fire pouring from his eye. My white hot magic screaming from my body. I steadied my breathing and forced my voice to stay even. "I don't want to argue with you, Balor."

His entire body sighed in relief. "And I don't want to argue with you. Can we go to our flat upstairs and talk all this through? I know you're worried about the others seeing you, but Elise has done a bang up job with your glamour. You can move back in. There's no need for you to stay in the safe house anymore."

I closed my eyes and shook my head. "Not yet. I need to take care of something first."

He furrowed his brows. "Don't tell me you've come up with another ridiculous plan to kill Nemain." His eye widened. "You're going to the Ivory Court, aren't you?"

"Not exactly." Slowly, I stepped off the stone dais and met him halfway across the floor. "Listen, I can't tell you what it is, or this isn't going to work. Can you trust me?"

He sucked a sharp breath in through his nose. "Clark, I don't like this."

"Do you trust me?" I asked again.

He pursed his lips, stared deep into my eyes. Finally, he nodded. "As long as you promise you won't go to the Ivory Court."

A slight smile flickered across my lips. "That I can promise you."

"Good." He pulled me to his chest and wrapped his strong arms around my body. My heart thudded loudly against my chest, in time with his. He felt so good, warm and strong and solid. So real. Nothing like the wraith that haunted the past. He was not Baleros. He couldn't be. He may have been reincarnated with the smiter's eye, but he hadn't gotten his soul. The Balor who held me close to him would never fight for darkness.

He pulled back and searched my face. "Should I be worried?"

"No," I lied through my teeth. "Just wait for me in the penthouse. I'll be up there soon."

He hesitated, just for a moment, and then he was gone, leaving me in my empty throne room with no one else but my past selves to keep me company.

~

There weren't many hiding spaces in a throne room and for good reason. Rulers did not enjoy being surprised by lurking guests. It was more than a little dangerous, providing hidey holes your enemies could utilise. Throne rooms were open, light illuminating every surface from the wide windows that stretched up to the arched ceiling.

But I was Clark Cavanaugh, and I knew how to hide. I found a small slab of stone in the far back corner, placed some drapery stylishly over it, and ducked behind. The moments stretched into hours. The light began to dim. Doubt started to creep in right about the time that my hunger gnawed a hole in my stomach.

We'd set the trap, but Nemain wasn't dumb. She'd proven that much time and time again. She might be vicious, angry, and horrifyingly good at the whole murder thing, but she was not low in the IQ department. That, plus her skill at reading someone's future intentions...well, maybe she'd guessed this trap, even though it had been sprung from a random moment and a random thought hastily pieced together.

After what felt like years, my eyelids began to slip downward. Sleep tugged at my tired brain, and my aching body begged for sleep.

And then the door banged open.

Footsteps echoed on the stone floor. In an instant, I was wide awake, shaken out of sleep with far more force than ten gallons of coffee could ever do. I pushed up onto my knees, staying low in a crouch. I listened hard as the footsteps grew louder.

She was approaching the throne.

I peered out of the slight opening between the drape and the stone. My heart banged so hard against my lungs that it was so loud, loud enough to drown out the footsteps drawing closer and closer to the large crimson skull throne that lurked quietly in the growing darkness.

"And there she is once again," Nemain whispered. For a moment, I thought she was talking about me, but then she kept her gaze tight on the throne, a creepy smile lighting up her face. No, not me then. She was talking to the bloody throne.

"I have missed you, my love." She caressed the bones, much like I'd done only hours before. That made a shiver course down my spine. "The Morrigan thought she could take you away from me, but she was wrong. The truth about her and Balor was too much for her pretty little half-fae head to handle. I thought

I'd at least have one battle on my hands, but we won't even have that. Shifters." She snorted. "You can never depend on them, not even as enemies."

Hot blood roared through my veins as my entire face went hot. I was so fucking tired of all the anger toward shifters. So much so that I wanted to abandon my post and confront her right here and now.

But I couldn't let her get to me. She was wrong about shifters, about my little half-fae head. And she'd find out soon enough.

With a deep breath, I ducked beneath the other side of the drape and disappeared out the door that she'd left cracked behind her. Elise was waiting, nervously striding back and forth along the corridor.

"She's in there, isn't she?" Elise asked in a low whisper. "She actually came?"

I nodded. For once, Nemain had played right into our hands. After so long, trying and failing to stay one step ahead, it was almost too hard to believe that we'd managed to reel her in for once. She had not anticipated a damn thing. And we were finally going to end this once and for all.

"Is everyone ready for the trap?" I asked.

"Yep, they're in position." Elise swallowed hard and wrung her hands together nervously. "You sure this is going to work, Clark?"

"No, I'm not sure at all." Better to be honest than anything else. We might have lured her here, but now we'd have to find a way to take her down. And only a few of us could do that. Me, Ronan, and Tiarnan. The only three who weren't under her spell.

"You don't think Balor should be here to help?" she continued.

"I wish he could be," I said.

But I didn't trust our combined power together in that throne room, even against an enemy. Not after the prophecy, not after what I'd seen the originals do to their world. I couldn't do anything that would jeopardise the lives of everyone who lived in this realm, even if that might mean we'd win against Nemain just a little bit faster.

Because winning wouldn't mean a damn thing if everyone was dead.

"He's going to be shitting bricks when he finds out you took her on by yourself. You know that, don't you?"

"I have a good reason. He'll understand when I explain it to him."

She gave a nod, but she didn't look convinced. She'd been his second-in-command after all. Hiding things from him wouldn't feel right to Elise.

"Just promise me one thing," she said in a whisper. "Be careful. You know how tricky she is. There's no telling what she has up her sleeve, and I'd hate to see anything go wrong. I know we've only known each other a few months, but it feels like it's been years. You're more than just my Queen. You're one of my closest friends."

I smiled, tears welling up in the corners of my eyes for reasons I didn't understand. There was no reason to be upset. Everything had gone exactly according to plan. "We'll be careful. I promise."

Tears slipped down Elise's face. "Okay. I'll give the signal."

But before she turned to alert the others who were hiding in wait for Nemain's arrival, she rushed forward and wrapped her arms tight around my neck. The scent of lilacs drifted into my nose, but also something else: fear.

"Don't be afraid," I whispered into her silver hair. "It's going to be okay."

"I hope you're right." She pulled back, turned her face away, and rushed down the corridor. My heart thumped right after her. After everything that had happened these past few months, I didn't blame her for being afraid.

Shouts echoed from deep within the Court. I turned toward them, expecting Ronan and Tiarnan to come charging my way. But it wasn't two sets of footsteps I heard rushing along the marbled halls. It sounded like the whole bloody Court.

18

Hundreds of stomping boots rushed my way, the sound filling my head like a swarm of angry bees. All the blood drained from my face, and I stumbled back a step, and then another. My eyes went wide; the floor beneath me felt like sinking sand.

Something had gone very wrong.

That was not the sound of an intricate trap springing into motion. That was the sound of a hundred fae with a mission.

And that mission was to kill me.

Everything within me wanted to stand my ground. I didn't want to run, and I certainly didn't want to hide, especially not when Nemain was right through those doors. It would only take a moment to end this now, though I'd been planning on my backup to be there with me to see this one through.

Sure, I was a pretty powerful fae, but I wasn't an idiot. I grew stronger every day, and more in control over my ancient powers, but I was still learning.

Where the hell were Ronan and Tiarnan?

I took one last look down the rumbling corridor, flicked my eyes toward the double doors that led into the throne room, and ground my teeth together.

Fuck it. This might be the last chance I got. Besides, I was glamoured. If they were storming through the corridors to find Clark, they wouldn't succeed.

I pushed open the double doors and slid back into the throne room.

Nemain sat on the throne, twirling one of the crimson skulls in her hands. Her lips twisted into a smile when she saw me. "Welcome, Clark. So good of you to join us."

My heart fell out of my body and hit the floor. It was a moment before I could find my voice. "I'm sorry. You must be mistaken. My name is Norah. I heard there was something going on in here?"

"Nice try," Nemain said, her smile never wavering. Instead, she twisted to the side and flicked her long, manicured fingers toward the corner. Elise shuffled out from the shadows, her head hung low. My hands curled into fists as I watched her climb the dais and stand by Nemain's side. Her cheeks were dotted pink; her entire body trembled.

"Elise?" I whispered before I was able to stop myself.

"That's right," Nemain said. "Your little friend here has given up the goose. Did you really think you'd be able to trap me? Inside a Court full of fae who are bonded to obey my every command? And here I thought you were smarter than that."

I wet my lips. Elise kept her eyes on the ground.

My heart hammered hard as my mind spun through the last few moments we'd spent together. She'd tried to warn me, in the only way she could. She'd tried to tell me how much she cared because she knew she'd have to betray me only seconds later.

Nemain must have gotten to Elise since I'd read her mind in the pub. I should have seen this one coming—I'd lured Nemain here after all. And once she'd arrived, she'd made her move before entering the throne room. The whole time I'd been hiding… Nemain had been whispering her orders into every fae's ears.

I couldn't hate Elise. Not for this. It wasn't her fault. I'm sure Nemain wasn't banking on that though.

"Fine. You caught me." I kept my gaze locked on my friend. "Elise, you can drop my glamour now."

Elise didn't even flinch in my direction.

Nemain's smile widened. "Elise won't be following any of your orders from now on. She reports to me and me alone."

"Only because she is forced to," I said, narrowing my eyes. "What kind of ruler can you truly be if the loyalty of your subjects isn't voluntary?"

"The successful kind." She leaned back into the throne and crossed her legs, drumming her fingers against the skull. "Elise, you may drop Clark's glamour. We wouldn't want the Crimson Court fae to be confused about her identity, now would we?"

Magic flickered across my body, a soft caress full of remorse. I looked down at my hands and saw my own. I was Clark again. For better or worse.

"That's pretty rich," I said, strolling closer to the throne. "Making some mind-controlled fae do your dirty work for you. Or are you too scared to try to take me on by yourself? I mean, I would be, if I were you. Last time you lost."

She hissed, and her eyes went as narrow as a blade. "I know all about your plan to use the wolf beast and the outcast fae against me. Don't act as though you were brave enough to fight me on your own. Elise told me every detail of your plan. All of it. I even know that you and your beloved Balor are at odds. Too worried he'll try to steal the throne away from you then? The honeymoon is already over?"

Hmm. Interesting. She didn't mention his eye. Did that mean Elise found a way out of telling her that tidbit of information? It was a pretty big bombshell. Literally. If Nemain knew, she would have probably led with that.

That meant we still had an edge, even if I didn't want to use it. If only I could get word to Balor, we might be able to turn this thing around. She wouldn't see the fire coming…

But could I really do this? Could I ask him to use his power, even knowing what could happen if he did?

The sound of thumping footsteps shot through the thick double doors that shielded the throne room from the outside world. The fae of the Crimson Court were coming to kill me, and Nemain once again sat on the throne. There was no saving the world of the fae unless I called to Balor for help.

I would just have to make sure that no matter what happened, we could not turn on each other. This fight was against Nemain. Not amongst ourselves.

I steeled myself as I closed my eyes and called upon the magic inside of my mind. I had spoken to him like this before. I had to pray it worked once again.

Balor. I need you. Nemain has me trapped in the throne room.

I wanted to say more, to explain to him exactly how and why this had happened. But there was no time for that. When I used my mind reading powers, I was too zoned out to protect myself. And if there was ever a time I needed to fight, it was now.

When I reopened my eyes, I found Elise staring my way. Immediately, she cast her gaze aside. I wanted to reach out toward her and pull her back in for that hug. I hadn't known what it had meant at the time, but now that I did, I never wanted to let go.

"I don't blame you, Elise," I said out loud. "It's not your fault."

Nemain narrowed her eyes, and the skull stopped spinning in her hands. She shot a sharp gaze toward my friend, and her lips curled. "I see what you're trying to do. You're trying to get inside her mind. It's pointless, Morrigan. Nothing you can say or do will get her to help you."

That wasn't what I was trying to do at all, but it was interesting to see that Nemain had no concept of genuine friendship. Not a surprise, based on what I'd seen from her in my past lives. She'd always been plotting, always been looking for the best way to get to the next rung on the ladder. Every ally was someone she could later stab in the back.

The doors flew open, and the Crimson Court fae piled inside the throne room. I jogged a few steps back until I was only a few meters to the side of the dais where Nemain was now holding court. My heartbeat practically throttled me with its speed, but I held my ground. The fae looked confused, angry, hurt. But they were not rushing at me. Not yet anyway.

They all gathered in a cluster in the center of the floor, looking at where Nemain, Elise, and I were gathered at the front of the room. This wasn't all of them, but it was a lot. Over half of the entire building was here. But, if I knew Nemain, the rest would be on their way soon.

I flicked my gaze toward the double doors. Where the hell was Balor?

"Welcome, my dear Crimson Court subjects." Nemain placed both feet on the floor and hurled a skull right toward the crowd. They screamed and jumped back, and the bones cracked on the stone, the pieces scattering wildly throughout the room.

"That right there was a dear old friend of mine," Nemain said in a bored voice. "Balor smited him and took his skull for his throne. You can still see the char if you look closely enough. Balor tried to paint over it, but it's beneath the red."

Right. So, Nemain had a grudge that went deeper than power.

Speaking of Balor? Where the hell was he? Despite everything we'd been going through, he would never ignore a call for help. And it only took a moment to get from the penthouse to the ground floor.

Worry crept into my heart like a poisonous spider, whose fangs were poised right over my veins.

Balor was missing, and Ronan and Tiarnan were nowhere to be seen. I hadn't spotted Moira or Kyle either.

ALL'S FAE IN LOVE AND WAR

Everyone I knew, love, and trusted were either missing or up on that throne held captive in Nemain's snare.

And a whole crowd of fae were just waiting for the word from their Queen. All she had to do was flick her fingers, and they would murder me.

"Clark," Elise suddenly whispered. "You have to get out of here. Now. She knows about the prophecy, and she's going to force you and Balor to fight."

All the blood drained from my face. "What?"

"Elise!" Nemain's voice boomed against the wall as she suddenly stood from her seat and grabbed my friend's neck. Her fingernails sunk in deep. Elise's eyes went wide as her entire body stilled. Nemain tapped her fingernails against Elise's skin, leaning in to whisper into her ear.

"I have no idea how you were able to do that, but I will not allow it again. You will obey me. You will *not* speak to Clark."

Elise's eyes fluttered like a butterfly trapped in a cage. Gritting her teeth, she hissed. "The Ivory Court turned her down. In favour of you. She wants everyone to see how terrible your power is, how much damage it can cause. Then, she can be the saviour, and you'll be gone."

Nemain let out a vicious growl, dug her fingers deeper into Elise's neck. And then she ripped her hand sideways. Blood spurted against the crimson throne. Elise's body fell, crashing hard on the stone floor. I stared, mouth agape, my mind barely seeing.

Elise was dead. She had sacrificed her own life to save mine.

As the world began to rush in around me once

again, I could hear Nemain's cackle echoing throughout the throne room. She stormed toward me, her arms outstretched to dig her nails into my flesh next. The puzzle pieces finally slid into place. She'd set another trap.

Me vs. Balor Beimnech.

Without another moment of hesitation, I transformed my limbs into wings and soared away.

19

I didn't get very far, but I didn't need to. As soon as I reached the roof of the building, through some clever flying through air ducts and vents, I shifted back into my fae form and sobbed until I had nothing left inside of me to sob. Heavy drops of rain pounded against my body as I peered through my soaking hair. Everything inside of me hurt.

Elise was dead. And it was my fault she'd been killed. I'd wrapped her up in my plot against Nemain, and she'd paid the ultimate price. If she hadn't tried to warn me, if she hadn't fought so hard against the bond, she'd still be alive.

I couldn't breathe. I could barely even think. Shivering on the rooftop of the old Battersea Power Station, I was alone, scared, confused.

Elise was dead. And it should have been me.

*H*ours passed before I was able to pull myself back together again. I couldn't shake the image of Elise crumpling to the stone floor, but my skin was growing numb and my body so chilled that I was certain I would never be warm again. It was time to get down off this roof, find somewhere dry with heat, and figure out where I was going to go from here.

With a deep breath, I transformed back into my bird and flew to Ronan's warehouse. No one was home, but I still knew his security code so I let myself inside. I took a quick hot shower, found a clean pair of sweats and a t-shirt several sizes too big, and shoved my iceberg feet into a thick pair of socks. Sighing, I took a look around. The place was still a mess from the fae who had broken down the door a few nights back. He'd only had time to replace the door and not much else. His computer monitors had been smashed, and the cage had been tipped to the side.

Still, it was a warm, relatively safe place where I could think.

First up, I needed to find out if anyone else escaped.

I dialled Moira's cell. It was a risk, but it was one I was willing to take.

"Clark, where the hell are you?" she asked in a hiss when she picked up only half a ring later.

"I can't tell you that," I said. "Where the hell are *you*?"

"I'm currently hiding in the fucking library with Kyle. We're going to try to get to my sword and then put a stop to this shite." A beat passed. "We saw everything go down on the security cameras, Clark. We were on the way to help, and then some bloody Fianna swarmed the command station."

She didn't mention Elise. Did that mean she didn't know? My heart squeezed tight. Moira needed to know. They were almost total opposites, the pair of them, but they'd had a bond, a real one, unlike any I'd ever seen. And I couldn't tell Moira what had happened over the phone.

"You know I want to believe you." I shook my head. "No, wait. I don't. Sounds like you've had a hell of a night that I wouldn't wish upon anybody."

A sigh. "No, I get what you mean. You want to trust my words, that I'm not currently under Nemain's bloody mind control bond."

"Have you seen or heard from Balor? Tiarnan? Ronan?" A part of me hated to ask, for fear of finding an answer I didn't want.

"Word is they've all been captured," Moira said. "Though how the hell the Fianna could take on Balor, I'll never understand."

Especially now that he had his eye again. I would be far more worried than I was, but I could still feel the magic of our bond pulsing between us. He was alive, and he was fine. He hadn't come to any harm. Yet.

"I want you to come meet me. You and Kyle. No one else."

"I'm pretty sure I can get to my sword," Moira argued. "And then Kyle will help me sneak into the throne room so I can kill Nemain."

I closed my eyes, breathing in the rugged scent of Ronan's fresh clothes. "You can't, Moira. She'll see you and stop you and twist her words into your brain. Hell, she'll know what you want to do, and she'll be planning for it."

Moira muttered a curse. "I would never willingly follow her orders. It pisses me off that I'm forced to listen to her damn words."

"Me too." I could hear Kyle's voice in the distance. "I follow Clark and Balor."

How I wished that were fully true. "So, you'll sneak out and meet me?"

"'Course we will," Moira said. "Tell me where and when, we'll be there."

I rattled off an address to her and glanced down at Ronan's oversized, rumpled sweats. "Think you could grab me some clothes on the way? Some of yours are fine if that's all you can manage."

Moira didn't ask why, for which I was grateful. I didn't want to explain that I'd sat on the rooftop naked for hours, crying over my dead best friend. With a lump in my throat, I hung up the phone and got ready for the next stage in my plan.

~

There was one hard lesson Nemain had taught me. I couldn't trust anyone, not even my closest confidantes. Not while she still breathed in the air of the Crimson Court. I gave Moira and Kyle the address of the old pub I'd crashed in the night Aed had chased me through the woods. Sheila was as accommodating as ever, and I paid her double her rate in order to occupy the room for a few hours. There were a few benefits to this set-up. One, we were away from the city, the Court, and Nemain. Two, no one was sneaking up on me out here in the middle of nowhere. If an army came running, I'd see them long before they reached me. And third…well, the old eavesdropping slats in the floor were about to become very, very handy.

I'd just settled in when Moira and Kyle pulled up outside of the pub. Moira climbed out of the car, her sword visibly attached to her waist. I watched them through the tiny window on the floor above, barely letting my eyes peek over the frame. Moira scanned the pub top to bottom, and her scowl deepened. On the other hand, Kyle was as white as a ghost. She motioned for him to follow, and the two of them headed inside.

"Well, now we're here," Moira said as she settled in on one of the barstools, glancing around. "This place is a shit hole. Why the hell did Clark want us to meet her here?"

"This is near the Lake of the Dragon's Mouth," Kyle said. "That night she got attacked. I bet she came here."

"Ah." Realisation dawned on Moira's face. "So, she's been here before. That means she knows the place. No doubt she's hiding just out of sight, waiting to read our minds."

"I wish she wouldn't read mine," he said quickly. "Won't the security tapes I brought along do just fine?"

Moira pursed her lips. "She'll want to watch them, but no, they won't do. Not after Elise betrayed her."

"Elise didn't betray her," Kyle said, his voice more

insistent now. "She wasn't in charge of her own actions. It's not her fault."

Moira gave a dismissive wave of her hand. "Elise has a strong mind. Stronger than most. Clark might forgive her, but I won't be that easy on her. She turned her back on us all."

My heart pulsed. They really hadn't seen the whole thing go down then. The Fianna must have interrupted before…Elise died. Swallowing hard, I decided it was about time I got this over with. Before I could talk myself out of it, I threw my thoughts forward and into Moira's mind.

I dove deep into her head, making certain to push past the lighter thoughts. Her mind was strong and firm and unwavering. She hadn't been compromised by Nemain. Smiling, I turned my mind toward Kyle.

I don't want to be the one doing this. Why couldn't have Nemain ordered someone else? I'm rubbish at this.

Fuck.

Gritting my teeth, I grabbed the cell and dialled Moira. I saw and heard her answer at the same time.

"Yo, where are you?"

"Act normal. Don't let your face do anything weird. Pretend you're a spy and that your enemy is on to you."

A beat passed in slow motion. Moira didn't move, didn't blink. Finally, she spoke, keeping her voice steadier than a heartbeat. "You want us to meet you somewhere else? Come on, Clark. Surely here's as good a meeting place as any."

"Good. Say something about me spotting another car following you. So, we need to go to another location, after you lose them."

Moira stiffened and cut her eyes to the door. Kyle frowned. "Damn. I didn't notice a tail. You got another address for me? *Or should I just knock the asshole out?*"

"No," I said quickly. "Don't knock out Kyle. It's not his fault. I don't want to hurt him. We'll go to the Lake of the Dragon Mouth. He can't get into contact with anyone once he's there."

"Yep, you got it." She gave a nod. "We'll be careful."

When Moira slid her phone into her back pocket, Kyle jumped off his stool and frowned. "What's going on? Why are we leaving? Is something wrong?"

"We've been tailed," Moira said in a tight voice. "Gotta get moving just in case it's a Fianna."

She clapped Kyle on the shoulder and steered him toward the door. "Come on, mate. We wouldn't want to do anything to jeopardise the mission, now would we?"

Kyle merely swallowed, his face just as chalk white as it had been when he'd come in. I should have noticed right away that he looked too nervous. We'd always gotten along. He'd even spoken up to me when he didn't agree with my commands. There'd been no reason for him to look as though he were walking straight to his death. Unless he was hiding a secret— Nemain was controlling his mind.

Slowly, she was chipping away at my support system, claiming them one by one.

The door suddenly flew open, and Sheila stood before me with a freaking mace club in her hands. She narrowed her eyes, looked me up and down.

"I thought there was something fishy about you

when you showed up here in the middle of the damn night, stinking like horse shit. Now, I know why. Your little friends are fae. That means you are, too."

Oh, great. Not this again. I'd been so wrapped up in taking down Nemain that I'd almost forgotten about the strained—to put it mildly—current relationship between humans and fae. Some of them hated us. Turned out Sheila was among them.

"I'm only half-fae," I said, like that would be enough.

Her scowl only deepened. "Half or not, you're important enough for there to be a reward out for your death. Story on the news said you're worth a hundred thousand quid."

20

A reward. Out for my death. Now, Nemain had a bounty on my head, and she'd passed it along to the humans as well. Wonder what the Circle of Night thought of this newest development. Would the greed in them put them after me, too?

"You don't want to fight me," I said quietly, holding up my hands. "Because you're right. I am fae. That means I have fae powers."

She snorted. "Go on then. Give me what you got. I'm in debt up to my eyeballs. If I go, I go. If not, well, that hundred thousand quid will get me out of the hole."

I wasn't surprised to hear she was struggling. Both times I'd been here, she'd only had a couple of patrons darkening her door. Of course, that didn't mean I was just going to stand here and let her kill me.

For the second time that night, I shifted into a bird and fled.

I perched on the edge of a branch, watching Moira and Kyle pick through the forest. No one had followed them, and Moira hadn't let him use his cell. He might very well have a tracking device somewhere on him or on the car, but there wasn't much we could do about that now.

When they were mere steps away from crossing the boundary into the Lake, I flew down from my branches and shifted just before them. Kyle shielded his eyes away from my bare form, his entire face as red as a rose.

"Ah." Moira tossed me a pair of her clothes—skin tight black pants, long-sleeved black shirt, and some black combat boots that were made for kicking ass. "You should start keeping outfits stashed around the country just in case."

Quickly, I changed into her clothes and felt a little more like an actual person now that I wasn't dragging around a loose pair of sweats. "Thanks for coming. Sorry it's been a bit all over the place."

Kyle kept his gaze averted. "We want to do everything we can to help."

"Good," I said, pressing my lips together. "Then, you'll come with me."

Together, the three of us stepped out of the normal world and into the Lake of the Dragon Mouth. The slashing wind and light sprinkle of rain halted immediately. In its place was a cool breeze, a sun that warmed my skin, and the soft scent of lilacs in bloom. Eyes wide, Kyle stepped forward, taking it all in.

"I read your mind back in the pub, Kyle," I said

quietly from behind him. "That's the real reason we're here. I know Nemain got to you before we did."

His face paled even more. With his tongue stuck out between his teeth, he grabbed his phone from his pocket and started to dial. I didn't make a move toward him. The Lake of the Dragon Mouth did not have cell service.

"You won't be able to make a call," I said, gazing around at the sparkling green, the deep blue hues, the golden light streaking through the cloudless sky. "I don't really understand this place, but I don't think it's even on the same plane of existence as the rest of the mortal realm."

He took a step back. "You're scaring me."

"Good." I gave a nod. "Then, maybe you will listen to me."

"I can't, Clark," he said, his voice in full agony. "You know I can't. Hell, I can hardly stand here talking to you. My order was to call Nemain, immediately, if you ever found out."

He twisted toward the tree line, and I shot out my hand. But I didn't have to make a move myself. Caer appeared, seemingly from nowhere, and stood right in Kyle's path.

He let out a guttural scream and stumbled back, his eyes as round as saucers. "You brought me here as a sacrifice to Caer."

"No, little duckling," Caer said, her thick dark hair rippling in the soft wind. "She brought me here to keep an eye on you." Her eyes flicked to my friend, my warrior. "Hello again, Moira."

Moira's eye flashed. "Caer. I hope you don't plan

on bestowing any more of your bloody prophecies today."

"For you, not today." Her eyes flicked to Kyle. "But perhaps to this one."

My curiosity was piqued by Caer's words to Moira. Hello, *again*? Did that mean Moira had been here once before? She'd never mentioned a prophecy to me, but I hadn't really wanted to tell anyone about mine either. Caer didn't deliver the kind of news that people liked to share.

I'd have to ask her about it later.

Right now, we had work to do instead.

"You can give a prophecy to him if you want, but I'm afraid Moira and I can't stick around," I said.

"No," Caer mused. "I suppose not. You have to go to Faerie."

"Say what now?" Moira asked. "Aren't we bloody well in Faerie now?"

Moira meant the mortal realm. Some fae liked to call it Faerie, even though it was the furthest thing from the truth.

"She means the old Faerie. The immortal realm. Our home."

Now, it was her turn to sport a blanched face. "But it doesn't exist. Those are just legends, old tales."

"Come with me," I told her. "And you can see for yourself."

ALL'S FAE IN LOVE AND WAR

"Bloody hell," Moira muttered as we stood surveying the hellscape that had once been the Faerie world. "You weren't kidding when you said it was destroyed."

"Unfortunately."

She turned to me, her golden eyes flashing. "What caused this? And why are we here?"

"We're here because I want you to understand the full weight of what we're up against." I levelled my gaze at her as a strange breeze that sparked of magic ruffled the hair trailing down my back. "How much did you see back at Court? How much did you hear?"

"I saw that you were surrounded, but the Fianna broke through the command station doors before you escaped." She rested her hand on the hilt of her sword and squeezed tight. "I still can't believe Elise turned on you."

I glanced down at the ground, and then lifted my eyes so that she could see the sorrow inside of me. "Elise fought hard against the bond Nemain holds over you all. She managed to warn me about a few things, even against Nemain's orders."

Moira's eyes slightly widened. "She did? That's my girl."

"The Ivory Court turned Nemain down. Said they want to show fealty to the Morrigan." I sucked in a deep breath, steadying myself, and then I plowed forward. "Nemain wants to pit Balor and me against each other, so that our power will threaten the world. When the other Courts see the horrible truth of me, they will turn their backs on the Morrigan and join Nemain instead."

Moira shook her head. "I don't understand."

"You see all this." I spread my hands wide at the ashen landscape before us. "I caused this. With Balor. Back when this all first started, the first Smiter and the first Morrigan were at odds. When they fought, their powers slammed together and caused the entire world to fall apart. Nemain wants to see it happen again, so she can swoop in and show the rest of the fae that she's the only one they can trust."

Moira let out a low whistle. "Damn."

"Moira." I took her hand, the one wrapped around her sword. "There's something else I need to tell you. Nemain didn't let Elise's rebellion go unpunished."

Moira's neck bobbed as she swallowed hard, and when she spoke, her voice was rough. "You mean, she sent her to the dungeons."

I squeezed my eyes tight and shook my head. "No. She did far worse than that."

"Fuck!" Moira screamed and ripped her hand out of my grasp. She stalked away, her entire body trembling with the kind of energy that could tear down a whole world. She stormed back and forth, from one end of the ashen hillside to the other. I stayed silent where I was, letting Moira deal with her grief and anger the only way she knew how.

She didn't sob on a roof in the rain like I had. She shouted at the heavens and pounded her fist against the ash.

In the end, we stood together, watching an alien sun rise slowly in the amber sky. At long last, she finally spoke again. "Elise was the closest thing to a sister I've ever had."

"I know," I said quietly. "I'm so sorry, Moira. It happened so fast. There was nothing I could do."

"Well, there's something we can do now," she said in a harsh whisper. "We'll avenge her death. By killing the one who murdered her in cold blood."

My heart thumped hard. "We can't go rushing into the Crimson Court. We have to be more tactical than that."

"Oh, we will be." Moira turned to me then with a grin. "You know why no one knows this portal to Faerie exists? Why everyone thinks it's all legend and myth?"

"I'm assuming it's because most of the fae who once lived here died in the blaze. Only a few made it to safety."

"Well, there's that, but there's also the fact that the legend says the portal was shut." She glanced behind her, at the rippling air that led back to the Lake of the Dragon's Mouth. "I don't think that's a lie. I think it *was* shut. And I think someone reopened it again."

"Okay…" I said, crossing my arms over my chest. "That could very well be true, but how will it help us defeat Nemain?"

"We find out how it got opened the first time, we lure Nemain here…" Moira shot me a wicked grin. "And then we trap the Faerie Queen in this realm. Forever."

21

It wasn't a terrible idea. The problem with Nemain was, she could see any direct attack coming from five miles away. The plan wasn't perfect.

"If we trap her here, instead of killing her, the fae of the Crimson Court will always be held to the magic of her bond," I said. "They'll never be free."

Moira arched a brow. "Maybe bonds don't work through different realms. How's your bond with Balor feeling? Still as bloody strong as ever?"

My interest piqued. When I'd first gone through the portal to Faerie, Caer had mentioned that the magic didn't work through the veil. It was why I didn't have access to those memories.

Frowning, I focused on that ever-present tug I felt deep within my bones. I barely thought about it now. It had begun to feel like a second skin. I closed my eyes and drew upon the magic in my core, waiting for it to flood over me like it always did. Usually, it pulled me under until I could barely breathe.

But nothing happened.

I felt empty. Alone.

My eyes flew open. "I don't feel it anymore." And then panic began to set in. "You don't think it's broken, do you?"

"Broken? No. We're no longer on the same plane of existence. I just don't think the magic can reach through the portal. "

I let out a breath of relief. "So, as long as Nemain can never again reach the mortal realm…"

"We'll all be safe."

Kyle jumped up from the dirt bank and brushed off his jeans. "Did you really go to Faerie? What did you see?"

"Sorry, mate," Moira said, clasping his shoulder. "We're not going to tell you a damn thing. Caer, think we could speak for a moment outside the earshot of this one?"

Caer pursed her lips and the space between her eyes pinched tight. She didn't like taking orders from anyone, least of all a lowly warrior fae. Caer was a goddess, the last remaining in this world. Once, there had been many just like her. Druids, they'd called themselves. Now, there was only Caer.

"You brought me no gift this time." Those words were to me.

"Our visit was a bit of a last-minute decision."

"I am aware," she said with a sniff. "Emergency at the Court. Everything is falling apart, right on time."

I narrowed my eyes. "What do you mean it's right on time?"

"You will see."

When we reached the little hut that Caer called her home, she ushered us inside to a cluster of short, wood-carved stools that sat around a tiny fireplace. I shot a glance at the open door where Kyle kicked several pebbles into the lake.

"Do not be concerned with the young fae," she said in a lyrical voice. "He does not wish to leave, therefore he will not flee. Nemain's orders cannot reach him anymore."

I let out an exhale of relief. Well, at least that was one less thing to worry about.

"We have a couple of questions for you," I began, but Caer held up a hand to stop me.

"You wish to know if I reopened the portal to Faerie. I can answer that easily enough. No, I did not. I merely guard it."

"*Can* you reopen it?" Moira asked, leaning forward as she braced her arms on her knees.

"I do not know how," Caer said. "You best consult with a mage. They created the link between the mortal and immortal realms in the beginning, after all."

I wrinkled my nose and glanced at Moira. "A mage?"

"I believe they call themselves sorcerers," Caer added.

Sorcerers. My stomach dropped through the floor. Sitting back in my seat, I let out a low whistle, letting the full truth of what she'd said wash over me. If we wanted to go through with this plan, we would need to once again befriend the sorcerers. And I'd been burned too many times by them before.

"Seriously?" Moira asked. "The sorcerers are

JENNA WOLFHART

humans. There has to be another way. Surely a fae is the one to close that portal."

"They are mortals who have been touched by the magic that seeped from the immortal world, your world, and into this one through the ley lines. That unique combination of being of both worlds is the reason they are able to control the portal."

I slumped back into my seat. Everything Caer had said made sense. Humans touched by magic. So, now we just had to find a sorcerer who wouldn't run screaming in the other direction, but also one who wouldn't zap us on the spot. This was going to prove to be interesting.

"We don't know any sorcerers who don't also want to fight us," I said.

Caer lifted a messy brow. "Oh, but you do. You may have forgotten him because you once thought of him as dead. Indeed, he is alive and has been hiding in plain sight."

I leaned forward, breath caught in my throat. "Jake is alive?"

"Motherfucker," Moira said.

We drove back to London in silence. Both of us were suffocating under the knowledge that had been draped over our bodies like heavy blankets. It was stifling. I wanted to scream and get out.

"So, maybe we don't try to trap her in Faerie after all," I said, tightening my grip on the steering wheel as I glanced at Moira.

She stuck her hand into a bag and munched on the few remaining salt and vinegar crisps left in the packet. "Just a little stabby stab? I'm down for that."

I blew out a hot breath. "Think we could get close enough to her to do it?"

Moira was silent for a long while. Only the crunch, crunch, crunch of crisps over the sound of the rushing wheels on the slick ground. I began to think she'd forgotten I asked a question.

"I keep thinking of plans, but then I realise we need other people to do them," she said, her voice a little rough. "A lot of times, glamour is involved."

I bit my lip to stop the tears from filling my eyes. "Kyle would also be useful. Tiarnan, too. Ronan, if only for his brute strength."

"Balor," Moira said. "His whole eye fire thing would certainly be useful." When I shot her a quick glance, she nodded. "Yeah, he told me he got it back."

"And see, that's what I don't get." I twisted the wheel, spinning the car around the sharp bend. "How the hell did he get caught? All he has to do is use his eye, and he's free. That's why he's so formidable. He just can't get caught."

My heart hurt just thinking about what Nemain might have done to get Balor in the dungeons. He would have to be unconscious. He would have to be in chains. Was he injured? No, that couldn't be the case. Balor had the power to heal himself. Besides, I kept checking on him through our bond, and he felt as strong and as powerful as ever. So, if he wasn't hurt, he had to be trapped some other way.

"I'm going to go out on a limb and say that we probably don't have much time to waste," Moira said.

"When we get back to London, we have to find that sorcerer."

I shook my head. "I can't believe he's alive. Balor was certain he died, transferring his power to Nemain."

"He's a tricky one. I never liked him."

"He might not want to play ball," I said. "Not if he faked his own death."

Moira scowled. "Then, we'll just have to make him."

22

The Cereal Killer Cafe was exactly the same as the last time we'd been here, minus the patrons making a line outside the door and down the block. Instead of the jam-packed atmosphere, the place was practically a ghost town now. Only one customer sat inside the sparkly booths. And that one customer was Jake.

"Look who it is." I slid into the seat across from him and laced my hands on the speckled table between us.

His eyes went wide, and he made a move to fly out of the booth, but Moira blocked his way, her fingers tapping the golden hilt of her sword. "I wouldn't try to run, cereal boy."

He wet his lips nervously. Now, he no longer wore his mage cloak or carried his staff by his side. Instead, he wore as nondescript clothing as possible. Jeans and a t-shirt. Nothing more. "Look, I'm sorry about what happened, but you have to understand."

"Oh, I understand." I leaned forward and stared

straight into his beady little eyes. "You tricked us all. You faked your own death."

He opened his mouth to argue, but then gave a little shrug. "You know what? I'm man enough to admit to that. I didn't want to die, so Elena helped me fake my death. She used another sorcerer's soul to give Nemain what she wanted."

Another sorcerer's soul? So, he'd let Nemain kill someone else just so he could survive?

"Man enough is one of the few ways I would describe you, cereal boy," Moira said in a low growl. She motioned for him to scoot over. He blinked up at her, sighed, and then shifted to the side, sliding his cereal bowl along with him. She edged into the seat, placing her sword squarely on the table so that the end pointed right toward his chest.

"Have you come here to kill me?" he asked frankly. "Because if you have, I would really like to finish my cereal first."

"We've come here because you owe us," I said quietly as the door chime rang, signalling another customer. "Would you agree with that assessment?"

"Yeah. Yeah, I'd say that's pretty true."

"Good." I grinned and leaned back in the seat. "Then, here's what's going to happen. You're going to find a spell for us, and then you're going to perform said spell. And you're not going to tell a single soul about any of this."

His face went pale. "Find you a spell? Again? But last time…"

"Well, you could do that or…" I flicked my eyes at Moira's sword, the sharp, pointy end still aimed at his heart. I mean, of course we weren't going to kill him.

He'd sold us out and then pretended to be dead, but I wasn't in the business of killing humans, magically blessed or otherwise.

"Right," he said nervously, clearing his throat. "The spell it is. But erm…you mind telling me what it is you're looking for? Because I can't promise you anything unless I have an idea of what you want."

"Sure." Moira and I locked eyes, and she gave a slow nod. "We want you to close the portal between this realm and the Faerie realm."

"Close the portal," he said with an eager nod. "Sure, okay. Easy, peasy. No big deal. None at all. That would definitely never kill an untrained sorcerer."

Jake jumped up from the table then and tried to squeeze past Moira. But she was like a rock. Hard and unmoving. She watched him scramble with an impassive look on her face, waiting patiently until he sighed and gave up.

He fell back into the seat and dropped his head into his hands. "You don't know what you're asking."

"Trust me," I said, voice going sharp. "I know exactly what I'm asking, and you're going to do it for us."

"I can't," he said in a whine. "It would literally kill me."

Moira arched a brow. "You seem certain of this."

"Of course I am." He glanced from Moira to me. "It's pretty much the biggest spell any human has ever cast. The guy, Nicolas Flamel, is infamous. *He opened a portal to another world.*"

My ears pricked up. "Nicolas Flamel? You mean the guy who searched for immortality?"

JENNA WOLFHART

"Yes." Jake nodded vigorously. "He searched for it. And he found it. In Faerie."

He must not have liked what he'd found because the guy was no longer alive. "Didn't that guy die?"

Jake practically jumped he nodded so hard. "A brutal death. From opening that damn portal."

Ah. Things were starting to click together now. Nicolas Flamel was alive around the time the fae had fled from our world and entered theirs. If he'd died searching for immortality in Faerie, it made sense. Hell, maybe he hadn't been killed from the magic at all. Maybe he'd been there when Faerie burned.

"Maybe the two incidents aren't related," I tried.

"Nope." He pushed away his half-eaten cereal, crossed his arms, and leaned back into the booth. "You aren't going to convince me of this one, Clark. No matter what you dangle over my head."

With a smile, I leaned forward. "What about that vampire thing, huh?"

Jake had first agreed to find the cure for the Sluagh—the walking dead, pretty much—in exchange for a little immortality of his own. He'd wanted to become a vampire. In the end, Matteo, the leader of the Circle of Night, had agreed, intrigued by the sorcerer's ambition.

I'd been pretty against it at the time. But I'd do anything now.

Jake drummed his fingers against the table, trying —and failing—to keep a neutral expression on his face. Finally, he slammed his hand on the table and cursed. "You bloody fae. I hate you, you know that?"

"Welcome to the club. Does that mean you're going to help us?"

"Make me a vamp first. *Then*, I'll close your damn portal."

∽

Outside, Jake insisted on having a smoke before we all piled onto the vampires' doorstep. Moira motioned me to join her a few feet away and hissed into my ear. "How'd you come up with that insane plan?"

"I winged it, to be honest." I shrugged, watching the sorcerer's hands shake as he lit his cigarette. "He doesn't think a mortal can survive the spell. So, let's give him a little help, shall we?"

"Vampires aren't exactly immortal," she countered.

"Close enough," I said. "They live through most things."

"And you think Matteo will go for this?"

"He was willing to go for it once before, and a hell of a lot less was at stake then." I pursed my lips, my mind on the strange, magnetic leader of the vampires. "Matteo is a lot of things. One of those things is bloody greedy. He enjoys his comfortable life up in his glistening London tower. I doubt he'd be too pleased if it got destroyed by a magical fire."

Still, Matteo often operated by his own rules. Luckily, I had something to offer him that I doubted he could refuse.

∽

We were welcomed into the lobby of the vampires' home base. They'd set up shop in the glistening Inside Out Building, previously home to Lloyd's of London, where floor-to-ceiling windows were blacked out to protect the vamps from the sun. The Lutine Bell stood proudly in the center of the floor, next to a Loss Book where the vampires recorded every negative thing that affected their lives. I wondered if I was in there.

Last time we'd come to visit the Circle of Night, Matteo had insisted the sorcerer stay out on the streets, though that might have had something to do with Balor's presence. The two did not get along these days, to say the least.

"Come with me," a polite, crisply-dressed female vamp said, motioning to the bank of a dozen escalators laid out before us. They criss-crossed up through the building like a maze of stairs. We followed her up to the second floor where we were shown to Matteo's expansive office.

He sat behind his desk, his hands folded over his chest. He wore his signature white suit, the smooth material draped perfectly over his strong but ancient form. His salt white hair had been cut short, highlighting the sharp curve of his jaw. When we strode inside, he flashed his fangs.

"Hello, Clark. And friends."

There was no smile for me this time. My heart thumped a little harder as I tried to think on the past few weeks. Had something happened to anger him that I hadn't realised? No. The vampires had been fine. Holed up in their headquarters mostly, but fine.

But there was that reward out there, that bounty over my head. Maybe he intended to cash in on it. Suddenly, I felt like we'd made a terrible mistake in coming here.

"Hello, Matteo," I said in a tight voice. "How's things?"

"You know, Clark," he continued as if I hadn't said a word. "I would feel much better about our relationship if you came to visit me more regularly. Perhaps at times when you are *not* in need. You only come to see me when you need something."

Ah. So, that was it.

I gestured to the plush seat that sat beside his desk. "Can I sit?"

"Yes, please." He held up a hand when the others moved to take the seats around me. "Just you though. I would like your guard and your…warlock…to remain where they are."

I glanced up at Moira, gave a nod. She nodded back. Jake stayed silent.

"I'm willing to admit you've got a point, Matteo. I haven't visited as often as I should. That said, I was under the impression the alliance between the two of us was broken."

"I see." He tapped his fingers against his chest, the chair creaking beneath him. "We may not have an alliance to fight side by side in a supernatural war, but we do have a friendship, yes? An agreement, of sorts. Otherwise, why would I not make a move to obtain that hundred thousand pounds Nemain is offering to anyone who kills you."

My eyebrows shot upwards. "So, you heard about the bounty."

"Of course I did. And I have not made a move because I thought we had an agreement."

"Isn't an agreement the same thing as an alliance?"

"Not in this instance. I am not against you, and you are not against me." He pressed up from his chair and braced his hands on his desk. "Now, why have you come to see me, Clark? I assume it has something to do with this sorcerer friend of yours. He's come to collect on his vampirism, I'm guessing."

"He's going to help us with Nemain. If you change him."

"I see." Matteo let out a laugh. "Because that little plan worked out so well last time. Tell me, Clark. Have you managed to round up all of the rogue Sluagh out on the streets?"

I frowned. "Some, but not all. The ones still out there won't survive long above ground. They'll decay soon enough."

We'd managed to track down some of the Sluagh that had escaped from the catacombs, thanks to Kyle's studious hacking of police reports. But we likely hadn't caught them all. Yet.

But this visit wasn't about the Sluagh, and he knew it. I didn't want to go into specifics with Matteo. We might have a friendship, or an agreement, or however he wanted to phrase it, but we most certainly did not have an alliance. I didn't trust him with the information on how we planned to defeat Nemain. He could very well be having similar meetings with her. And there was no way in hell we'd ever be able to trap her in Faerie if she got even a whiff of what we had planned.

"I'm here to make you a deal," I said.

"Well, well, well." With a delighted sigh, he eased back in his chair and crossed one suit-clad leg over the other. "Things certainly just got much more interesting indeed. What is it you wish to offer me, love?"

"The Mayor of London, yours to change."

23

Obviously, I didn't have Richard Longfellow, the Mayor of London, in the back pocket of my jeans, but I didn't think it would be terribly difficult to convince him that vampirism would make his life a hell of a lot easier. For one, he would have access to some pretty solid persuasion powers. That kind of thing is pretty valuable to a politician.

It was a move I'd been contemplating for awhile. If the Mayor decided to join the side of the supes, the streets would become peaceful again. He could convince the humans to stop coming at us with bats and knives.

Win win, as far as I could see.

Matteo let out a chuckle. "You certainly weren't kidding. That is the deal of a lifetime. What makes you think you can hold up your end of the bargain? Where is this lovely Mayor of yours, and how can you be sure you can get him here?"

"Longfellow is a man of ambition. Aren't most politicians?" I shrugged. "How could he refuse? Power, persuasion, wealth, and a lifespan that's much longer than he'd normally get."

Jake held up a hand. "That's why I'm here."

"A very good point," Matteo mused. "A very good point indeed. And you and your little fae army will allow it? Last time we spoke, Balor insisted that Jakey boy here would be the only human I change."

My heart pulsed at the thought. Balor hadn't seemed particularly thrilled when I'd brought up my Mayor idea to him before. And truthfully, I understood why. The vampires had ended their feast on humans many years before. We didn't want to go back to the time of midnight vampire killings. Not to mention the fact that many humans couldn't even survive the change to begin with. The Mayor could very well die from this. And *that* was a risk Balor didn't want to take.

"Desperate times. Desperate measures," I finally said.

"And your lover? Where is he?"

Currently trapped somewhere by my centuries-old enemy.

"He's busy."

Matteo let out another chuckle and laced his hands behind his head. "Very well. I suppose you are entitled to your secrets."

"I'll convince him that this was the right choice."

But would I? He'd worked so hard to convince the vampires to control their violence toward humans. The last thing he wanted was for it to begin again. Would this be yet another thing that could cause strife between us? Would it be *the thing* that would set off the spark to end the world?

"Good." His smile widened. "Now, go get me the Mayor. Your friend can stay here."

"But…" Jake glanced from me to Matteo back to me again.

I stood from my seat. "We'd like for you to go ahead and change Jake first. Then, I'll go get the Mayor."

Matteo's eyebrows winged upward. "That would be silly on my part. How will I ensure you give me what you've promised?"

"Because I am giving you my word. We've made a deal."

"A fae's word means nothing."

Matteo stood from his chair and stalked over to Jake, who took two small steps back. His face had gone a shade too white, so pale it matched the vampire's hair. His entire body trembled, fear and excitement flickering in his eyes. He wanted his immortality so terribly, but it also scared him to death.

It should.

The vampire's arm shot out. He had Jake against his chest faster than I could blink. Fangs flashed beneath the golden light. The pointed ends tore through the flesh of Jake's neck. Blood spattered on the floor around them as Matteo drank deep.

Moira shifted toward them, her hand on the hilt of her sword. I held out an arm to hold her back, waiting, my heart roaring in my ears.

Matteo pulled his mouth away from Jake's neck and licked his blood-stained lips, revealing the wound he had left behind. It was as large as a golf ball, wet and raw and soaking red. No human could survive that kind of wound.

I shook my head, horror churning through my gut. What had I done?

"There. The change has been started for your precious sorcerer. The rest must happen fast or Jake will die. Bring me the Mayor. Now. Or I will not let your sorcerer live."

"What a wanker," Moira fumed as we stormed out the front doors of the vampire trade center. It had only taken us moments to rush down through the escalator maze and out through the lobby, but it had felt like decades. Jake's life was hanging in the balance. If Matteo did not feed the sorcerer any of his own magic-tainted blood, Jake would die.

I wet my lips and tried to get my bearings. We were smack dab in the middle of the City of London, and we needed to get to the Mayor. Luckily, Mansion House was close by, the official residence of the mayor. I pointed my feet in the right direction, and motioned for Moira to follow.

"Come on, let's go."

We reached the Mayor's house in no time. A large rectangular stone building that echoed the ancient architecture of the older parts of London. There was no time to stop and admire it though. I grabbed Moira's arm and pulled her through the door, taking us straight to the front desk. A woman waited there for us, her sleek brunette hair cut short at her shoulders. Her wide rimmed glasses sat perched on her crooked nose, making her look like a quirky librarian.

"Yeah, I'd like to see the Mayor," I said, heaving out the words through belabored breaths.

The woman frowned and took a long while to examine me from head to toe. She probably wasn't terribly impressed by what she saw. I was still wearing Moira's outfit, which was too tight in some places and too large in others. Her waist was thinner than mine, but her glutes and quads were noticeably more muscular. And with my sweat-soaked forehead, and the hair plastered to my face…yep, we were definitely getting in to see the Mayor.

"Do you have an appointment?" she asked.

"Erm…yes," I tried. If I said no, she would most likely dismiss us immediately, which would give me no chance to scan her mind. I needed to hand this over to Moira, who could keep the woman talking. All I needed was a few moments to pluck out a thought that could get us inside.

Moira cleared her throat. "Mr. Longfellow and I go way back. My parents are good friends of his. We dine with him often for afternoon tea. Did you know that his favourite snack is a little sandwich square with cucumber and butter?"

Where the hell had that little story come from?

I dove into the assistant's mind. Her thoughts were fluttering and flying all over the place. Unease slithered through her like a snake. There was worry here and fear and something else. A massive need to spill a bunch of tea.

Not the drinking kind.

These girls obviously don't have a meeting with the Mayor, and I'm dying to ask them why they're looking for him. Do they know something about his disappearance? Should I ask them about it? He hasn't been seen in five days. All the staff say we shouldn't go to the cops, just in case he's gambling like he did back when he first got elected.

Well, that was certainly an interesting development. First off, it was news to me that Longfellow had a gambling addiction. But that wasn't even the juiciest part of these revelations. The Mayor was missing. But who the hell would've taken him?

The assistant's thoughts continued to churn through her mind like a hurricane.

He never should have gotten tight with those werewolves. They're not trustworthy. I told him that at the start. Still can't believe they came storming in here, hauling the Mayor out of his chair like he was nobody at all.

I pulled out of her mind, having heard everything I needed to understand exactly what had happened here. For some bizarre reason, the shifters had returned to London, and they'd set their sights on the Mayor. They'd taken him. To where? I was pretty sure the assistant didn't know. She sounded scared and confused, like she wanted to go to the cops but she didn't want to get the Mayor in trouble. Just in case that old gambling problem was back.

After smiling and coming up with an excuse to leave, Moira and I ducked out of the building. What the hell were we going to do now? Richard Longfellow was our ticket to Matteo completing the change for Jake. And, without him, we had no other way to close the portal.

As much as I hated the Mayor and what he had done to the supernaturals of the city, I had a feeling I was about to go save his life.

24

"I didn't know the Pack was back in town," Moira said when we ducked into the doorframe of an abandoned storefront. A heavy mist had blanketed the city while we'd been inside, transforming the streets into a smudged painting.

I leaned against a flyer that advertised an upcoming gig in the club across the street. "Neither did I. They haven't made contact."

"Not even with Ronan?"

I shrugged. "They're not particularly close. If he knew, he would have mentioned it. They probably knew he wouldn't approve of this whole kidnap the Mayor plot they have going on."

Moira scowled. "Bloody shifters." Then, she slid her eyes my way. "Obviously, I don't mean you."

"Bloody shifters," I agreed.

Moira sighed, scanned the streets. Her entire body trembled with barely-contained energy. She was desperate to do something, anything. The two of us were alike in many ways. We didn't like to stay still for too long. We liked to jump into action. Sometimes, that worked out pretty well. Other times, it led to disaster.

"Does this mean our whole portal closing plan is off the board?" she asked.

That plan had been her idea, and I knew she wanted to see it through.

"The shifters have the Mayor. That's not a great development for anyone, ignoring the fact we want to take him to the Circle of Night." I shook my head. "What are they going to do with him? And what if the humans of the city found out? It wouldn't take much for news to spread. His assistant in there sounded desperate to share. It won't be long before she spills it to someone."

Moira's body practically rippled with anticipation. "So, we go and rescue the Mayor from the Pack."

I couldn't help but let out a strained laugh. "We go rescue him from one band of supernaturals so that we can deliver him to another."

"Damn." Moira nibbled on her bottom lip. "When you put it that way…"

My heart squeezed tight. I understood what she meant. We saw ourselves as the 'good guys' in the fight, but were we just as bad as Nemain?

"We're letting the Mayor make a choice about his fate," I finally said. "I don't know what the shifters are doing to him, but I doubt it's voluntary."

Moira nodded slowly. "The man making our lives miserable will have a choice, unlike the rest of us. That's good enough for me."

We had next to no idea where the Pack had stationed themselves in London this time. After taking a quick drive by their old warehouse in the middle of the docks, we quickly realised they'd found somewhere else, probably for this very reason.

They didn't want anyone to find them.

"What the hell are we going to do?" Moira threw up her hands after we'd checked out a few more warehouses in the area, just in case.

I tapped my fingers against the steering wheel. "I could find them. But I need access to my PI stuff. Or I need a Kyle."

"Pretty sure Kyle's not happening, not unless we want him to lure us to our deaths." Moira leaned forward and cranked up the heat. The chilly night had fallen as we'd searched for the Pack, and the cold air seeped into the car. "He's smarter than we are. We'd end up in chains before we even knew what hour it was."

"You've got a point." I pursed my lips and stared out the front windscreen at the hulking warehouse before us. "So, I'm going to have to do a little PI work, the old-fashioned way."

"How? I thought all your computer stuff was destroyed when the humans trashed your old flat."

Only a few weeks ago, Nemain had tracked down the old flat Balor had kept as a safe house, just in case I ever needed to escape there. It ended up we *had* needed to escape there. Unfortunately, I'd had too many ties to the place, and we'd eventually been found out. Nemain had leaked our location to the humans, and they'd swarmed in with bats and knives.

The whole placed had been destroyed. Poor Henry, my old landlord, was still cleaning up the mess. I still needed to make it up to him somehow.

"That's why we're going to have to do it the old-fashioned way." I shifted the car into drive. "We're going to the cops."

~

Moira had to stay in the car. Unlike me, there was no mistaking that she was a fae. There was an ethereal presence about her. Glowing skin, brilliant golden hair, and sharp, pointed ears that stuck through her thick strands. Plus, she refused to go anywhere without her sword.

I waltzed on into the place like I'd been there a million times before. In truth, I'd been here three times. Twice in undercover mode to weasel out some info. And once to get Balor out of jail. I had to hope they wouldn't recognise me this time. I'd shoved a woollen hat onto my head. It didn't hide my red hair completely, but it was all we had.

The overhead fluorescent lights cast everything into shades of yellow. I strode up to the reception desk and smiled down at the small squat man who chattered into a phone about a supe who had crashed a pub downtown. I bit the insides of my cheeks, crossing my mental fingers that he wouldn't look up and see fae, that he would see only human.

He set the phone back into its cradle and shifted his attention to me. "Yes?"

"I need to speak to someone about a crime."

His eyes went narrow. "This isn't really an office

ALL'S FAE IN LOVE AND WAR

for that kind of thing. You're better off going to the main station."

"But you're the place that deals with those supernaturals, right?" I asked as sweetly as I could handle without gagging.

A strange expression flickered across his face. "Who told you that?"

"I saw it on the news." Figured that was a pretty easy lie. The news liked to leak everything.

"For fuck's sake," he muttered beneath his breath with a sigh. He pinched the bridge of his nose, and I swore he counted to ten inside his head. I wasn't reading him yet, but I already knew how he thought. "Of course they did."

"I hope I'm not in trouble." I picked up a pen on the desk and began to fidget with it. "I just saw something pretty terrible and thought I should tell you guys."

Whoops. My American slipped out just a bit then. It was hard to keep up the fake accent sometimes. Thankfully, he didn't notice.

"Look, this isn't normally how we do things around here, but I'll take your information and pass it along." He picked up a pad and clicked open his pen.

Bingo. I had him now.

"This is going to sound a little crazy…" I began, trying to get into the whole role as human without a clue.

"Trust me. We've heard it before."

"Right. So, I was walking home in East London, and there were these guys…" I shook my head. "Not guys. Monsters. Like, werewolves. Their bodies were covered in fur, and they were howling."

The pen clicked, and he stopped scribbling. "I see."

Quickly, I dove into his head.

Another false report. I'm getting bloody tired of these. Now that the supes have come out of the proverbial closet, every single idiot in this city is coming out of the woodwork.

I pulled back out of his head and frowned. I needed to get way more than that. How could I convince him that I hadn't come up with some kind of conspiracy theory? Sprinkle in a little of the truth.

Leaning forward, I dropped my voice to a whisper. "Look, I know it sounds crazy. But werewolves. In East London. I thought they lived in the docks."

His eyes slightly widened, and he clicked his pen again.

Maybe this one might be on to something.

That was it. Nothing more. Man, this was going to be like extracting teeth.

"What makes you think they lived in the docks?" he asked, his pen poised over his notepad.

"My uncle works out there. He's seen them. Says they mostly keep to themselves. One time, I was out there picking him up after his shift, and I saw a couple myself. That's how I knew what I saw tonight."

"In East London, you say?" He scribbled onto his notepad. While he was distracted, I tried one last time.

"Yeah. Shoreditch."

Strange they're running about in Shoreditch. Mayor made a deal they'd keep to themselves. Stay out of London. Live in those damn forts.

Forts? What forts?

Still can't believe he spent all of that taxpayer money on doing those things up again, fixing all those damn stilts. For supernatural scum. Those old things aren't even a part of bloody London.

I knew what he was talking about. During the Second World War, the UK had built Navy forts in the Thames estuary a couple hours outside of London. Steel and concrete living quarters held up by stilts. They'd been abandoned for years.

Until now, apparently.

With a smile, I nodded, realising he was still looking at me. "Is there anything else you need from me?"

"I asked what time you saw them." He blinked at me. "You okay? You zoned out there for a bit."

"Yeah." I gave a little shiver. "Guess I'm still a bit freaked out by the whole werewolf thing."

"Understood. Just tell me what time you saw them, and you can be on your way. Oh, and let me get your name and number, just in case one of the case officers wants some more details from you."

"Of course." I rattled off some false information. Obviously, I wasn't going to give him my actual name and number. And then, before he could realise he'd been duped, I was back out the front door.

When I slid into the car, Moira was waiting, heat cranked up to max. "So? Any luck?"

"The Pack made a deal with the Mayor, and they've relocated to those old World War II forts out by Southend-on-Sea. Apparently, he put some money into it for them. Got some renovations done."

"You mean those old things on stilts that look like rusty boxes?"

"Those are the ones."

"Damn." She let out a low whistle. "They probably love that. They're secluded, probably self-sustaining. They're out of the way of the war. No one will bother them there. No fae, no vamps, no humans." She twisted toward me and frowned. "But if the Mayor pretty much gifted those old forts to them, how the hell did that lead to this whole abduction thing?"

"That I don't know. The cops aren't aware he's missing just yet."

"How'd you find all that out anyway?" she asked.

"I made up a story for the guy at the desk and listened in on his thoughts."

She arched a brow. "And that's old-fashioned, traditional PI work?"

I shrugged and put the car into drive. "It is for me."

25

*B*ecause of traffic on the A13, the drive over to Southend-on-Sea took well over two hours. By the time we'd arrived, night had deepened well past midnight. The moon hung low in the sky, and clouds skittered along the horizon. A few stars dotted the inky blue above, visible now that we'd inched away from the London smog.

The forts themselves were in the sea just beyond East Beach of Shoeburyness, a town within the borough of Southend-on-Sea. We parked and made our way down the wooden steps to stand on the pebble-covered sand. The tide was out, and a long stretch of sand disappeared into the night. Small boats were dotted around the beach, tipped sideways, waiting for the water to return.

In the distance, right at the horizon, sparkling lights illuminated mushroom-shaped objects, barely visible to the naked eye.

Moira tsked. "So, they're all the way out there, huh? Don't suppose you know how to sail."

"I know how to fly," I said.

"Clark," she said, voice rising. "You can't go out there by yourself. There's no telling what you'd be walking into."

I gave her a frank look. "I certainly can."

She sighed. "Fine. Wrong choice of words. You can do whatever you damn well please, but it's not the brightest idea in the world for you to go out there without backup."

"You're not wrong. I shouldn't." I gestured at the expanse of sand and water before us. "But do you have any bright suggestions on how we can get out there without my wings?"

Moira pointed at one of the capsized boats. "That right there."

I arched a brow. "We're going to drag that thing all the way out to the water? And somehow manage to get to the forts, even though neither of us know how to work a boat?"

I blew out a breath and considered my options. Flying would be the quickest and easiest way to reach the forts. Problem was, I'd have no backup. I'd also have no clothes, and I didn't love the idea of fighting a bunch of werewolves buck naked. And, if I left Moira out here on the beach by herself, I'd have no way of knowing if Nemain's lackeys would burst out of the bushes and whisper orders into her ears.

I let out a heavy sigh. "We'll take the damn boat."

There were several sailboats scattered around the sand, but Moira and I chose a much simpler option. A rusted old yellow boat that could only be powered with oars. There were two wooden planks nailed precariously to the inside, seats warped with age and damp.

A chain was attached to the front, leading down to a rusted metal anchor. It was held in place with a lock, but Moira made quick work of it with her sword. Together, we hoisted the thing onto our shoulders and began the trek through the water-logged sand.

My feet sunk into the ground as the boat weighed heavily on my shoulders. I had to stop several times to catch my balance, coming far too close to splatting face first into the ground. Moira grunted, muttering beneath her breath about bloody shifters and Mayors who wanted us all dead.

Finally, we reached the water. The boat slid from our shoulders, as we both sighed with relief. When it hit the sand hard, water and dust sprayed into our faces. Salt stained my lips.

We slid the boat into the sea, climbed inside while it haphazardly shifted from one side to the next. I took the front and Moira took the back, an oar each.

My boots were soaked through, and my socks were drowning in cold water. Shivering, I turned the oar from side to side, digging it deep into the water. From behind me, I heard a rhythmic splash as Moira did the same. It took several tries for us to steer the thing in the right direction, but soon, we found our rhythm, and the boat spun through the sea.

After what felt like hours, the mushroom-shaped forts grew larger before us. There were seven of them, vast and rusted metal hulks that cowered precariously on stilts. Catwalks led from one to the next, a maze of metal amidst the sea.

Our boat slid next to the closest fort as we steered

toward a platform that served as a dock, one surrounded by several other boats.

"I think we're here," I couldn't help but say out loud, even though I was merely speaking the obvious.

The looming, decaying presence of the forts was kind of creeping me out.

We came to a stop just in reach of the platform and jumped out before we could spin away. As soon as we did, the boat began to drift, abandoning us for the safety of the waters.

"Traitor," I muttered to the thing. Now, we'd have to find another way to get the hell out.

Something to worry about if we managed to escape.

First, we had to find the Mayor.

I pointed to a rickety ladder that led up to a door in the bottom of the hulking fort. "Ready to go up?"

Moira wet her lips, her hand finding comfort in the golden hilt of her sword. "I've never been more ready."

And so we climbed.

The ladder shook as we scaled our way up to the entrance to the forts. I reached the top first, and pushed open the door. I steeled myself before I poked my head through. We had next to no information on how this place worked. What kind of guard system did they have in place, if any? What kind of weapons did they use? Had they seen us arrive? Would we trip some kind of alarm?

After a few moments passed with nothing more than the rattle of the ladder drifting on the salt-soaked wind, I pushed through the hole and rolled into a crouch. I found myself in a dimly-lit room. The entire

ALL'S FAE IN LOVE AND WAR

thing was filled to the brim with old, rusted machinery that hadn't seen the light of day in decades. No shifters. Nothing other than a thin coating of dust.

Moira joined me in the room and glanced around. "Not exactly what I was expecting. Thought you said they fixed this place up."

"There are seven of these things, and they're pretty damn big. My guess is they picked one and went with that. Probably the one in the center. That's the one I'd pick if it were me. You could expand outward, and set up security around it, if anyone found out where you were."

"Think they've seen us?" she asked.

"Maybe," I said. "We'll find out soon enough."

Together, we inched our way through the cluster of machinery until we came to a rusted metal door. Holding my breath deep in my lungs, I twisted the handle and pushed open. Another room, much more dust. This one held next to nothing in it. But it was the only way out.

We threaded through the maze of rooms until we finally found ourselves peering through a window that looked out onto a rusted, flaking 'balcony' that shortly connected with a catwalk. The catwalk itself was…interesting.

It reminded me of a swinging bridge, wooden planks separated by at least a foot. Two thin ropes hung freely in the wind on either side. All it would take was a little stumble, and you'd fall into the churning waters below. And these forts poked high enough out of the water that it would hurt, at the very least.

"There's got to be another way," Moira muttered

beneath her breath as she stared at the rickety catwalk.

But my attention had been dragged upwards to what looked to be a second floor of the fort across the way. The windows were lit up, and shadowy figures moved behind thin, gauzy curtains. Music pumped out through tinny speakers. The shifters were inside. We'd have to cross this catwalk if we wanted to reach them.

"Look." I pointed through the cracked window to show Moira what I'd found.

She peered through, frowned. "I think I see now why they chose this place. No one in their right mind would come all the way up here and climb across that bridge."

"I guess it's a good thing we're not in our right minds."

Despite her visible unease, Moira laughed. She shook her head and motioned at the door. "It's a damn good thing. Go on then. Let's open her up and get to the fun part."

The fun part, I assumed, was taking the fight to the Pack.

With a deep breath, I pulled open the heavy door. A loud creak echoed in the dank, musty space, a sound I was sure would carry to the fort next door. A light wind ruffled my hair as I stepped out onto the little rusted platform. It was just about big enough for the two of us to stand.

The bridge stretched out before us, beckoning us to cross. It looked sturdy enough for approximately one werewolf. I had to assume the Pack chose to rarely leave this place. Otherwise, it'd be a major pain in the ass.

"I'll go first," Moira said as she began to step forward.

I blocked her way. "No. I will."

"You're my Queen," she began.

"Exactly," I said. "*I* protect *you*."

"That's actually not how this whole thing works."

"It does with me." With a deep breath, I took a timid step forward before Moira could stop me. I understood her point, and my memories backed her up. Queens and Kings typically had their royal guard. They were sworn to protect the crown, no matter what, against all threats. If the Queen's life was at risk, the guard went down first.

But I wanted to do things a little differently. I wanted to lead by example. I wanted to stand at the front, and not behind.

The bridge swung beneath me as I took one slow step after the other. The thin, rough rope dug into my palms, I was clutching on so tight. The world seemed to sway beneath me; my head began to spin. When Moira saw me a quarter of the way across, she joined me on the bridge.

We were both halfway across when the door of the fort behind us swung open. A dozen shifters spilled outside, perching on the platforms, the bridge, some clinging to the side of the rusted steel beams.

I slowed to a stop, heart hammering in my chest.

And then I heard another door swing open. The one we'd left behind us.

Slowly, I turned, heartbeat pulsing in my neck. More shifters had spilled outside. They must have been waiting inside that fort all this time.

And now we were trapped on the bridge.

26

As far as I could see it, I only had two options. I could shift, fly away, and leave Moira to face this fate alone. Or, I could stand my ground.

Narrowing my eyes, I braced myself for their approach. Worst case scenario, I could use my powerful shout to knock them down. I parted my lips and called upon the power deep inside me, conjuring the magic that gave me my warrior scream.

Anderson edged to the front of the Pack, fur popping through the skin on his muscular back. "Careful there, Clark. You're in a precarious position. If you try your shouting spell on us, it'll break the damn bridge. If you try to fight us, you will lose your balance and fall. You cannot best us here. But it's your choice, of course."

I raised my voice to shout against the wind. "What makes you think we're here to fight you?"

"If you were here for a friendly visit, you would have come alone." He gestured at where Moira was clinging to the shifting bridge. "It would have been a lot easier to get here from the sky. Instead, you chose to bring your warrior."

"Things have gone a little pear-shaped in London," I shouted back. "I couldn't risk leaving her alone, where Nemain might get to her with orders that would turn her against me."

I could feel Moira frowning at the back of my head.

Of course, that wasn't the entire reason I'd brought her along, and I hoped she understood that I was blagging it a bit. I didn't want the shifters to think this was some kind of enemy invasion, even if it kind of was. I knew Moira wanted to charge and fight, but if we could get inside peacefully, we'd have a much better chance of making it out alive.

With the Mayor, who was probably their prisoner.

"Things in London have been 'pear-shaped' for awhile," he answered, flicking his fingers in quotation marks. "That's why we got out of that hellhole. Too bad Ronan just *had* to go back before we found a real home."

"Great place you picked," I said, trying to sound casual. "It's secluded. And since you've got seven of the things, there's plenty of space. It must be pretty run down though. There's rust everywhere. Can shifters get tetanus?"

He scowled. "You're not here to talk about tetanus, Clark. You're here to find out what happened to the Mayor."

I tapped on the rope bridge, gave a nod. "I wasn't going to lead with that, but yeah, I am here because of Mayor Longfellow. He's missing, Anderson. And his assistant had good reason to think it's because of you.

Now, maybe she's wrong. I hope to hell she is. But I had to come and find out."

"That's what I thought," Anderson said, motioning to the shifters who sat scattered across the fort behind us. "You should have stayed away, Clark. This business has nothing to do with the fae."

So, they did have him.

"What have you done with him?" I asked. "Please tell me he's still alive."

"Oh, he's still alive," the shifter sneered. "For now."

"Anderson. You're a smart guy, and you've always been reasonable with me. You've got to let him go."

"Nah, I can't do that," he replied.

"We won't be leaving without him."

"'Course you won't." He took a step back and gave a nod to the shifters. "Boys. Bring them in."

I braced myself on the rickety wooden planks as the shifters swarmed toward us from both sides. Moira grabbed my arm, her nails sinking in deep.

"I don't suppose you'll just hand the Mayor over and let us go?" I asked, trying to stall them so I could think up some crazy way to get us out of this.

"Nope, not happening."

The shifters stormed toward us. There wasn't much we could do. If I tossed my magic at them, I might be able to take them out. But I was pretty sure I would take *us* out, too. And I'd be okay in the end. I could fly away easily enough. But I wasn't going to risk Moira's life for a slim chance that I might not break the whole damn bridge.

When the closest shifter reached us, I threw out a fist and punched him right in the gut. Shouting in rage, he tumbled back. I grinned and bent my knees, waiting for the next shifter creeping toward me, the battle singing in my veins.

From behind me, I could hear Moira joining the fight, hurling her own fist toward faces, chests, and maybe even balls.

I got a few more punches in and several good kicks, but there were far too many of them versus us. They had no fear at all, crowding in on the bridge, even though the thing was groaning beneath our feet. Finally, I had to give up the ghost. We weren't going to fight our way out of this one.

"Moira," I called over my shoulder. "Let's stand down for now."

Immediately, she stilled, though I could still feel the energy radiating off her body. The shifters surrounded us. They grabbed our arms, shoved them behind our backs, and took us as their prisoners.

They escorted us into the fort. We passed several open doors, the shifters jerking us roughly down the corridor. The rooms we passed were just as rusted inside as the exterior walls. A dozen twin mattresses sat in a line on top of stained carpet cut into mismatched squares. A tiny table sat beneath a window edged in rust, where a thick pipe stretched in, connected to a wood stove.

Everything was faded, decaying, and stained. This might be the kind of home they'd always wanted—secluded, safe, fully theirs—but it was a fucking dump.

They shoved us forward, and I tripped along the warped floor until we came to a larger room. More squares of mismatched carpet had been spread across the floor, in puke green and orange hues. A circular oak table sat beneath one of the many windows, along with several kitchen chairs that looked as though they belonged in a middle school cafeteria. There were a cluster of sofas and chairs lurking around a coffee table covered in candles. In the corner sat an old white TV that must have belonged in the eighties. All the walls were covered in rust.

"Welcome to our humble abode," Anderson said, stretching his arms wide with a grin. "Red Sands Tower."

"Looks like it needs a lot of work," I said with a wry smile. "Unless your preference is decaying eighties aesthetic."

His eyes darkened. "Yes, I'm aware. You asked why I brought the Mayor here. This is why. We had an agreement, and he did not hold up his end of the bargain. He was to renovate this place. It is liveable now, but he swore to make it comfortable, too. Sand down the rust, install some new carpet, give us some fresh furniture to make it feel like home."

I nodded and glanced around. "Yeah, I heard he was doing the place up. Seems like the cops are pretty certain he used taxpayer money on it."

"Well, he hasn't spent a dime," Anderson said in a snap. "This is exactly how it was left, the same as it was back in the 60's when the pirate radios moved out. In fact, most of this furniture is the same. Hell, this is the only fort that is actually habitable. The rest of them need repairs. We were promised the whole lot."

"Pretty shitty," I admitted. "But surely keeping Longfellow here against his will isn't the solution. He can't buy paint from Homebase if he's your prisoner."

Anderson flashed me a smile. "He's just taking

some time out from his Mayorly duties. We're making him see things our way. When we're certain of that, we'll let him go."

I let a beat pass before answering. "What was your end of the deal anyway?"

"We promised we'd make things easier on him. We'd stay out of London and tell him everything we know about the supes." He shrugged. "That included information on you, love, I'm sorry to say."

Ah. So, the Pack had been informing on us, all the while holing up inside what I was sure they expected to be some kind of luxurious, renovated castle in the sea. Instead, they'd gotten a decaying hunk of metal.

No wonder they were pissed.

But I was pissed, too.

I tried to shove away from the shifter holding my arms, but I was held firmly back. Eyes narrowed, I lobbed my words at Anderson. "How dare you rat us out to the humans. I thought you were a coward when you ran, but you're far worse than I thought."

"Things are changing, love," Anderson said. "The only way we're going to survive the future is if we break free of the past. That means aligning ourselves with the humans now, not the other supes. I know you see it as a betrayal, but we're not blood. I have to take care of my own."

27

We let ourselves be taken through the maze of corridors until we came to a room guarded by two beefy shifters holding daggers in their fists. Anderson cracked open the door and ushered us inside. There, we found the Mayor. Longfellow was chained to a radiator that squatted beneath a small window. His head hung low to his chest, scraggly dark hair falling into his eyes, his chin brushing his stained shirt. Bruises covered his slack face, and deep purple spread beneath his eyes. With the greying hair at his temple, he looked sixty instead of forty-nine.

But he was alive.

Matteo was likely wondering where the hell we were. He'd threatened us with Jake's life, leaving his future hanging in the balance, waiting for his first taste of blood. I had no way of knowing whether Matteo had given him that precious life-force, or if he'd let him bleed out before him, his crisp white suit a contrast to the thick blood on the floor.

We hadn't come back. Not yet. Jake could be dead for all we knew.

But I had to keep pressing forward, hoping against all hope that Matteo would remember I'd always kept my word.

"You wanted to find the Mayor? Well, here he is." The Pack alpha slammed the door behind us and the lock clicked heavily into place. A moment later, I heard the murmur of voices as he gave his orders to the guards at the door.

I whirled to Moira, heart hammering. We'd done half of what we'd come here to do. We'd found the Mayor. But we'd also been trapped inside.

"We'll get out," she said in a hiss, eyes flashing. "But first we need to wake this asshole up."

I knew how she felt. The Mayor was not high on my list of favourite people right now. He'd negotiated with the Pack against us all, and he'd worked the humans of London into such a fury that they were salivating to see our blood painting the streets.

"Here," I said, pushing past her. "I'll try."

I gave the Mayor of London a hard slap on the face. An instant later, he sputtered, swallowing a lungful of air. He babbled incoherently, squirrelling around the floor in fear. He scuttled over to the corner and clung to the radiator, staring up at us both with wide, red-rimmed eyes.

But then he relaxed. "Oh." And then his eyes widened once more. "OH."

He recognised me then. I would hope he would. As the Mayor in charge of squashing the supernatural rebellion, he should be pretty up-to-date on the current developments at the Crimson Court. Especially since he'd been instrumental in sending a protesting mob to our front doors.

"You're the girl who took the throne," he finally said, voice scratchy, tired, and rough. "That half-fae."

My entire body bristled in response. "I'm the Morrigan, the current leader of the Crimson Court. You may address me as Queen."

His cheeks went pink. "I can't do that, or our actual Queen might decide to hang me for treason."

"I'm pretty sure Elizabeth is not that kind of Queen."

"No," he admitted. "But you are, I'm guessing. The fae are violent, vicious things. You should all be put down before you kill us all."

With a sharp laugh, Moira turned to me. "Why are we saving this asshole again?"

It was a really damn good question, and it was almost impossible to understand why we'd put ourselves through the wringer to get here. His hatred ran so deep. Maybe I'd judged him wrong. Most humans would kill for a chance at what basically amounted to immortality. Even the staunchest supporters of supernatural disdain would throw their lot in with us for the change.

But maybe we'd come all this way for nothing.

"I think he'll see things in a new light when he chats with the leader of the Circle of Night."

The Mayor sat a little straighter. "What's this about the Circle of Night?"

"Matteo wants to speak with you," I said, watching him carefully for his reaction. "I'm assuming you know who he is."

"Of course I do." His Adam's apple bobbed. "I've

been trying to get a meeting with him for months, but he wouldn't see me."

Probably something to do with you blasting your bigotry all over the news.

"Interesting." I crossed my arms over my chest. "I thought you hated supes. Why would you want a meeting with the head vampire?"

He gestured at the rusted lodgings. "Same reason I wanted to speak to the Pack. I'm ready to make him a deal."

"Ah. You want him to leave London, just like the shifters did," I said. "You want the vampires gone."

"That's pretty much the long and short of it, yeah." He brushed his scraggly hair out of his eyes. "If I can get most of the supes out of London, it'll be a show of strength for everyone else. The city's biggest problem will have been taken care of with no blood shed."

"Thanks to you," I added with an arched brow.

The pink of his cheeks deepened into red. "If the city wishes to thank me for my service, I won't deny them that."

"And what about the fae?" I couldn't help but ask. "You haven't come to us with one of your so-called deals."

He pressed his lips firmly together. "Hmm."

My heart thumped hard in my chest. Suddenly, his face closed off, his eyes went dim. He'd been happily chatting away until I'd brought up the lack of a deal with us. That meant only one thing. He was hiding something.

"Moira." I gave her a quick nod, and she understood me instantly.

Narrowing my eyes, I focused my mind on the Mayor before me, but before I could reach my power toward him, he held up his hands in surrender.

"I know what you're going to do. I've heard about your power, and I really don't want you to use it on me." He shook his head, his entire face turning the same shade of yellow as the rotting carpet.

I crossed my arms and leaned against the wall, and then thought better of it when rust rubbed against my arm. Pushing away, I glared down at him. "I want information. And I'm going to get it. Either you can give it to me willingly or I'll take it out of your mind. Your choice."

With a heavy sigh, he dropped his head into his hands. "I really, really hate you supernaturals."

"Well, you'll be pleased to know that the feeling is mutual. We don't much like you either," Moira said.

"Fine. Whatever." He peered up at me through his red-streaked eyes. "I haven't approached you because I reached out to someone else first. There was another Queen sitting on your throne when I began my negotiation plan. She was going by the name of Nemain. I realise she's not in London anymore, but she is intent on returning to her throne. And I made a deal to help her do that."

I narrowed my eyes. "Spill. All the details."

He sighed. "She's agreed to leave London for good, and she'll make sure no fae stay inside that old power station when she does."

Moira arched her brows. "That doesn't sound like something Nemain would agree to."

"Well," the Mayor said, wincing. "You're really not going to like this part. I told her that we would not force our hand in trying to get her to leave until she was ready. So that she can stay and take care of you, get you off the throne. So, there you have it. That's the deal."

So, the Mayor *had* made a deal, after all. It just wasn't with me. He'd somehow gotten to Nemain before I'd kicked her off the throne, and he'd been working on her behalf ever since. He would let her take care of me any way she saw fit, as long as she'd leave the Battersea Power Station free of fae when it was all over.

The fae of London didn't matter to her. They were merely a stepping stone to getting what she truly wanted: reign over the entire supernatural world.

"Well, then." Moira dropped onto one of the thin ratty mattresses and kicked her feet up to prop them against the wall. "Guess we won't be taking you to see the Circle of Night."

The Mayor pressed up from the floor to stand on wobbly legs. "Now, wait a minute. Let's not be too hasty. Surely we can come to some sort of understanding."

I arched a brow. "You really want to meet with them that badly, huh?"

"Out of all you supes, the ones the city fears most are the vampires," he said, brushing the grime against his oversized suit trousers. "Not you lot, even if you're the ones who have caused the most damage."

"Sounds like you're in a bit of a pickle," Moira said with a grin. "The Circle of Night ain't going to talk to you without our help."

"Fine," the Mayor said. "What do you want?"

Little did he know that what we *really* wanted was

for him to speak to the Circle. But it was better if he didn't know that he was playing right into our hands. Because then we could ask for more.

I exchanged a glance with Moira. "We want you to call off the human mob outside the Court. You'll have to make the call first. Tell them to stand down, and then we'll take you to the vamps."

His eyebrows pinched together. "We don't have a phone."

"Not yet." I nodded toward the window, and then grinned. "But we will as soon as we get out of this place."

His eyes widened. "You're going to break us out of this place."

"'Course I am. Did you think they were just going to let us walk out the rusted front door? We're their prisoners. The only way out is by force."

He nibbled on his bottom lip. "Maybe if you tried to reason with them."

"It's too late for that," I said. "And we don't have that kind of time. We're leaving *now*, and you're coming with us."

But Longfellow didn't look convinced. "Say you manage to pull this off, and we do get out of here. What's to stop these werewolves from coming for me again?"

I strode over to the Mayor and placed heavy hands on his shoulders, looking deep into his grey-streaked eyes. "Easy. You're going to give them the damn renovations you promised. And you're going to give it to them fast."

He yanked at his chains and scowled. "The City doesn't have the money for that."

"I don't care if you don't have the money. You'll have to bloody find it. You promised them a home, and you're damn well going to provide it."

He blinked at me for a moment, and then laughed. "I've got to hand it to them. Whatever magic they've worked on you, it's a hell of a potent combo. To think you could fight so hard for the ones who have imprisoned you."

Scowling, I poked my finger right into the very center of his chest. "Listen. I've given you a lot of slack here. I've come to save you, even when I shouldn't. You have no idea about the supernatural world. You don't know a thing about how we work. But you'll find out soon enough."

28

We waited until the distant voices disappeared into silence. The wolves had gone to bed, having enjoyed a night of howling at the moon. I supposed they enjoyed being out here in the midst of the sea. They didn't have to worry about their call to the moon drifting into the ears of nearby humans. They could be themselves, without fear.

It was a pretty sweet deal, when you looked at it like that.

I made the Mayor turn his back while I slid off my shirt and toed off my jeans. Naked, I transformed into my raven and edged out the cracked window, leaving Moira to watch Richard Longfellow. If I returned and found him with a bloody nose, I wouldn't be surprised.

The next few steps were tedious, when I was aching for a fight. I flew down to the boat that had drifted a mile or so away, rowed it over to the fort, and waited while Moira threw down my clothes. Dressed once again, I set my sights on the shifters.

They clearly had some sort of security set in place.

Most likely, they'd triggered the entry door with an alarm, or they rotated guards to keep out an eye for potential visitors. If I went back up the way we'd first gone inside, I'd no doubt find myself surrounded again.

I needed to get inside some other way, and I needed to find our weapons. Preferably clothed.

Frowning, I rowed through the waters until I was bobbing just beneath the hulking, rusted mushroom that was the Red Sands Fort. There was no platform here for docking boats, nor ladders leading up into hatch doors. If I wanted to get inside, I'd have to do it some other way.

My eyes scanned the building. The only thing that connected the water to the fort were the stilts. Swallowing hard, I rowed a little closer, eyeing up the four concrete poles. There were rusted pipes edging down the side of them, bolted on with several steel beams. On the underside of the mushroom fort was a crisscrossing maze of more pipes.

I had an idea. It might be a stupid one, but it might be the very thing to get me inside.

Rowing just inches away from the concrete stilt, I pushed up out of the boat and clung tight to the first steel beam that bolted the pipes into place. The floor of the boat dropped out from beneath me, and for a moment, my arms screamed in rage. But I clung on tight, determination churning in my gut.

I wasn't a full fae, but I was full grit. I wouldn't allow my weakness to let me down again.

After a moment, I began to climb. Up I went, gripping tightly to the pipe. It shuddered beneath me, the rough flaking rust scratching my palms. I grit my

ALL'S FAE IN LOVE AND WAR

teeth and continued. My legs were wrapped tight around the stilt, even though they barely went a quarter of the way around.

I didn't look down as I climbed. I could hear the water getting more distant, could smell the stench of sewage and decay as I got closer to the fort above.

Finally, I reached the top and looked across at the maze of pipes. They didn't look particularly secure. Several screws were missing, and they sagged toward the waters, like they were reaching out for relief.

With a deep breath, I plowed ahead. I had no choice but to continue. I'd gotten this far. Might as well keep going all the way.

I swung from pipe to pipe. My legs dangled beneath me. Every muscle in my body groaned. I hadn't done anything like this in my life. With a deep breath, I hauled myself over the ledge and collapsed into a crouch.

My breath puffed out of me, forming a thick mist in front of my lips. Heart racing, I shook my head. I could hardly believe it. I'd done the impossible. I'd scaled the fort and made it to the top.

And I didn't even need my damn wings to do it.

Maybe I was more fae than I thought.

Of course, it wasn't over just yet. I had to get inside, find my friend, and get the hell out of this dump. But before I did that, I had one last thing to take care of. I crept over to the catwalk, whispered a few words, and watched as the ropes frayed into ash.

And then the catwalk fell into the sea.

The dimly-lit corridors were quiet when I eased inside the fort. I'd climbed in a few doors down from where the shifters slept for the night. Sucking my breath deep into my lungs, I slowly eased myself down the creaking floor.

And came face-to-face with the two guards standing watch outside the prisoners' room.

"Oh." My eyes widened as I took them in. Our weapons were just beside them, propped up in the corner of the hall. I flicked my eyes from their faces to the door, and then to my sword.

Everyone sprang into action.

They drew their blades, positioning their muscular, thick bodies between me and my sword. But we weren't on a rickety bridge that could collapse into the sea. We were on solid ground. Curling my hands into fists, I called upon the power deep inside of me. And then I tipped back my head and let it out.

Pure white hot electricity shot from my throat as my scream filled up the silent night.

My power hit them square in their chests.

They fell, eyes wide and unseeing.

Without another moment of hesitation, I grabbed the swords and kicked open the door. The other shifters would have heard my shout, and they'd be on their way here within seconds. I rushed inside. Moira was already waiting, her eyes sparking with respect.

I tossed a sword to her waiting hand and nodded toward the open window. She grinned and stepped aside. And then I threw the Mayor of London out into the darkness of the night.

29

I dove after the Mayor, shifting my arms into wings to slow my fall, and then shifting them back just before I hit the water. I heard, rather than saw, Moira splash into the sea, having jumped just after me.

Tumbling through the water, I opened my eyes. The Mayor was sinking fast into the sea, his limbs slack, his body unmoving. Gritting my teeth, I swam after him. The fall had probably knocked the wind out of him, and he'd been left reeling. Down I dove until I reached his side.

I grabbed the Mayor and kicked my legs, forcing us to swim toward the surface. When my head crested the water, I sucked in a deep breath, my lungs stinging.

Moira popped up beside me, her golden strands darkened by the night. "I hope this asshole's worth all this."

"He will be," I promised, and I hoped I was right.

We hauled him into the boat.

The wolves appeared in the windows above, shouting down at us. Some were scurrying to the catwalk, the one that I'd destroyed. Smiling, we turned the boat toward the shore and began to row. They would no doubt come after us in time, but for now, we were safe.

When we reached the bank, Longfellow tumbled out of the boat and began to run on a pair of very wobbly legs. Moira cursed beneath her breath and launched after him. He didn't make it very far. He was weak, and very much human, and she almost ran as fast as light. She tackled him to the ground within seconds, and she pinned his arms to his back.

She leaned down, her wet hair dripping onto his cheek. "Nice try, asshole, but you're not getting out of this that easily."

~

Moira and I dragged an unconscious Mayor through the golden, gleaming doors of the Circle of Night. Getting him inside had been more than a little tricky. Obviously, everyone in London knew what he looked like. It was past three in the morning, but that didn't stop the partying humans from stumbling around London in their heels. We'd waited a full half hour before the coast was clear.

And then we booked it inside.

"Clark." Matteo dragged out my name as he appeared, seemingly from thin air. "I thought you weren't going to return. I'm glad to see I was wrong, though…he is in far worse shape than I had anticipated. What have you done to the poor man?"

ALL'S FAE IN LOVE AND WAR

"We brought you what we promised, but I'm not giving him up until I know you've held up your part of the deal," I snapped. "Where is Jake?"

"Your sorcerer friend is fine," he said with a dismissive wave. "He is resting. You'll be pleased to know that he survived the change."

Relief shuddered through me. As much as I hated to admit it, we needed that guy. He was the only one who could close the portal on Faerie, the only way we could trap Nemain in another world.

"When will he be awake?" I asked.

Matteo glanced down at his golden Rolex. "He'll be awake by sunrise, but he'll be weak. Best wait until sunset to have him do whatever it is he's promised."

"Good." I nodded. "Sunset will do."

Matteo's smile widened as he motioned toward the Mayor, unconscious and still hanging between me and Moira. "I would like my prize now."

Even though we'd gone to hell and back to bring the Mayor to Matteo, I had a sudden wave of hesitation go through me. The guy was an asshole. He'd said and done a lot of shitty things, and he'd sooner see me die than rule uncontested in the Crimson Court. But he was still a person, a living being who I didn't want to feed to the wolves.

Handing him over to Matteo required a trust I wasn't sure he'd earned. "How do I know that you will do right by him?"

Matteo's expression sobered. "Clark, my dear. It would not behoove me to mistreat him. We want him on side, do we not?"

After a moment of hesitation, I nodded.

"Then, trust me when I say no harm will come to

him. And if we truly do pull this off, and undo the damage he has done to the human perception of us, perhaps the fae and the vampires can find an alliance once again."

Hope sparked within me for the first time in a very long while. So much had gone wrong. So much had been lost. Nemain held the Court captive while Moira and I were out here flailing around with all the fight we had inside of us. Maybe, just maybe, we could turn this thing around. We had Jake, who would help us trap Nemain in Faerie, closing the portal shut behind her. We'd delivered the Mayor of London to Matteo, who would convince him to see the supernatural side.

All we had to do now was take the fight to Nemain.

"Oh, just one more thing," the white-haired vamp said, just as we turned to go. "I've heard a bit of information, and I thought it prudent to pass along."

I frowned, cocked my head. "What's Nemain done now?"

He winced. "I'm afraid it is not Nemain who has done the thing, but your Balor. Apparently, he has taken her side, his mind transfixed by a fae called Lizzie. He has vowed fealty to the self-proclaimed Queen. In return, she'll allow him to reign, as her proxy, over the London fae."

The floor became a vacuum beneath my feet, sucking me out of the present and into the past. Moments flipped by in quick succession. The smiter betraying me. The smiter loving me. The smiter stabbing me in the back. Closing my eyes, I gritted my teeth and forced my mind to focus on the here and now. But the blood roaring through my veins was too much for me to take.

This couldn't be right. It couldn't be real.

Balor Beimnech, the love of my life, had turned his back on me.

30

All I wanted was to storm the Crimson Court, plans abandoned, and confront Balor right here and now to find out the truth. Had he really bowed to Nemain? Had he really turned his back on us both? If it weren't for the past, I never would have believed it to be the truth.

But I knew what we were both capable of. I'd seen it with my own eyes. If any part of the smiter were still inside of him, I knew Balor could discard me for the crown.

"You need to calm down," Moira said, her voice even, steady, and as unemotional as a stone. How could she be okay with this? If he'd betrayed me, then he'd turned on her, too.

"How can I calm down when my mate has vowed fealty to our greatest enemy? The very fae who murdered his sister? The one who killed so many of his fae?"

I stormed up and down the block, a magical

billowing wind trailing behind me. Humans stopped to stare. For once, I didn't care what they thought.

"I'm sure there's an explanation."

I stopped and glared. "Is there? Because it makes far too much sense to me. No wonder he's been blocking me out of his mind, not answering my calls to him. No wonder I can feel him through the bond alive and unhurt. He's fine. He just doesn't want to risk me finding out what he's done."

"Balor would never bow to Nemain," she insisted.

"He might if it meant he could sit on that damn throne of his," I muttered. "We have to go confront him, and we have to do it now."

"Think about what you're saying," she said. "If you storm in there now, like this, you know what will happen."

She left the rest unspoken, but I understood in an instant what she meant. My magic was storming around me like a hurricane, primed and ready to clash against his. If I went in there this angry, this world could burn, just like Faerie had.

This was all part of Nemain's plan. Convince Balor to join her cause and let the information leak. She must have known that I had contact with Matteo. Why else would she let the information get back to him?

"You're right," I said, my body trembling from the force of my magic. "As much as I hate to admit it, I can't go in there like this."

"We should stick to the plan," she said. "We'll lure her out of there, and we'll trap her in Faerie."

Moira was right. I had to keep a tight grip on our

plan. We couldn't deviate, no matter what Balor had done. We would do what we'd come here to do, what we'd worked so hard for. The portal would close with Nemain on the other side of it.

But we would trap Balor in there, too.

We crouched in the bushes on the bank of the riverfront, watching the front door of the Crimson Court. Things must have gone pretty well with the Mayor, because the lawn was clear for the first time in months. Humans were not charging back and forth, waving their signs in the air and screaming about the sanctity of their streets.

Everything was silent, still, and calm. Except for the bloody sorcerer beside me.

He clapped his hands and grinned. "You have no idea how ready I am for this. I've never felt so fucking alive. I think I'm going to jump out of my skin."

"Please don't do that." I pinched the bridge of my nose. "Because then I will have to clean up a skin suit, which will be difficult to explain to the cops."

He made a face at me. "You're such a downer. Hey, maybe you should ask the vamps if they can change you. Trust me, it's like the best drug you'll ever do."

I exchanged a glance with Moira, who looked about as annoyed as I felt.

"Hey, friend," she said through gritted teeth. "While we appreciate your renewed zest for life, would you mind shutting it for a bit? We'd prefer not to tip anyone off that we're out here…hiding *quietly* in the bushes."

"Oh." He gave an eager nod. "Right." Then, he pulled an imaginary zipper across his lips, and smiled.

Why couldn't we have changed a more zen member of the sorcerer family?

"So," Moira said, blowing hot air onto her hands. "Place looks pretty quiet. No one is coming or going. No visible guards. It looks pretty peaceful for once. What do you reckon?"

"I reckon it's time we set our trap," I replied.

She gave a nod, punched a number into her cell phone, and waited. A moment later, she smiled. "Ondine, mate. You alright?"

A beat passed. "No, I'm not working with Clark. The bond with Nemain wouldn't let me if I tried. I've been trailing her, trying to figure out what she's up to. And listen to this, I think I've figured it out."

A moment passed, and then she smiled. "Yeah, wait until you get a load of this. She's gone to the Lake of the Dragon Mouth, and she's made a pact with Caer. Apparently, they're doing some sort of spell that will mold the Crimson Court crown—and the magic that goes along with it—onto Clark's head permanently. Once it's attached, there's nothing Nemain could do to get it off."

I bit back a grin. Moira was really getting into this. She would make a pretty damn good spy.

Her eyes went wide. "Yeah, I mean, I suppose beheading her *could* work."

Suddenly, my grin died. Moira flashed me an apologetic smile, but my heart clenched tight all the same. This was Ondine she was talking to. *Ondine*. I hated that Nemain had turned her so harshly against me.

A second later, Moira snorted. "I can't believe you don't trust me. I've got proof. Here, I'll send you a photo."

I'd taken a picture of the crown, in its little box, just in case I'd ever need proof of what I'd done with it. That moment had come far sooner than I'd expected.

In anticipation of this call, I'd shot the photo over to Moira's phone. While Ondine waited, Moira tapped a few times against the keypad. A moment later, I heard the *whoosh* of a message sending. She pressed the phone back to her ear.

"Sent. You get it?" And then she smiled. "Yep, that's right. I told you she took the crown to Caer."

Another beat passed, and a wicked glint echoed in Moira's eyes. "How am I supposed to know how a goddess's magic works? All I know is that she can do it. I heard them talking about it with my own two ears."

This was good. It sounded like Ondine was curious about this thing. I mean, why wouldn't she be? I'd stolen the crown from the Court.

"Oh yeah." Moira nodded, giving me a wink. "Caer was totally into the idea. Something about a prophecy, I don't know. It was hard to hear. I was hiding in the bushes."

Another pause.

"Yeah, you can't spit without hitting one of Caer's prophecies. Seems this one has to do with who ends up ruling the fae."

Moments passed while Moira nodded. I leaned forward, desperately trying to hear, but she shooed me away. After a moment, she made her goodbyes, her eyes dancing with pure delight.

She punched a button on her phone and smiled. "She bought it."

31

We watched the cars pull out of the Court, their tires skidding on the rain-slick ground. The mist that had covered London these past few nights had grown into a drizzle. We were soaked to our skin, but we were so caught up in our mission that we barely noticed. At least I didn't, and I was pretty sure Moira wasn't bothered herself. And the newly-changed vamp? He looked like he was enjoying the hell out of every single second that passed.

I pushed up from the ground. "That's it. The trap is set. You should get going."

Moira frowned. "Don't you mean that *we* should get going?"

"I'm going to follow the car in the air," I said. "Once she's within a mile of the Lake, I'll fly ahead to warn Caer."

Her expression darkened. "I don't like this. We agreed we wouldn't split up."

I took her shoulders in my hands and squeezed

tight. "And we didn't. We've made a great team, you and me. Thank you for standing beside me when no one else has. Trust me, I'll never forget what you've done for me these past few days. But I need to fly ahead. If Nemain gets there before I do, the trap won't work. I'll handle her until you get there, and I'll get her into Faerie. It's up to you to make sure that Jake is ready for the moment I jump out of that lake."

Moira nodded, her expression growing serious once again. Her eyes were shining, almost as though they were filmed over with tears. I'd never seen Moira cry. She didn't like to show her emotions to the world. But I could tell that my words had dug a little deep into her soul. I hoped she knew I'd meant every word of it.

"See you on the other side," I said.

And then I flew.

It was easy keeping track of Nemain's car. I just followed the pull of my bond. Balor was inside of it with her, his mind and body brimming with intense energy. As I flapped my wings in the sky above him, I tried to reach out and get a feel for his thoughts.

But that steel wall still stood between us, blocking me out.

When we were a few miles from the Dragon Mouth, I picked up speed and flew ahead. Caer was likely watching our approach with whatever goddess skills she had, but I wanted to warn her regardless and get Kyle the hell out of there. He was good at many a thing, but fighting wasn't one of them.

I flew straight through the trees and crossed the boundary before even bothering to shift. When I dropped to the ground, I changed into my fae form and glanced around.

Darkness swirled through the valley. Storms kicked up dirt and grass, yanking the multicoloured flowers from their stems. Caer stood in the center of it all, the twisting crown atop her dark hair, her arms outstretched toward me. Kyle was nowhere to be seen.

I approached her, my footsteps soft on the mossy earth. I'd known that she would not be pleased to see me, but I'd also known that she'd be expecting it. Caer had been playing her own little game, something I'd suspected for awhile. At first, it was not clear she held any cards to her chest, but I'd started to realise after some time.

She doled out information, only giving enough for the next step. And I'd played into it, every moment along the way.

"Hello, Caer," I said quietly, gritting my teeth against the onslaught of her power.

"You brought a war onto my doorstep."

"Yep. And you wanted me to do it."

Suddenly, her arms dropped, and the magic vanished without a trace. "Ah, you are more clever than I thought."

"Only a little," I said. "I only know that you've been pulling my strings. I still don't know why."

"You would not," she said dismissively before striding across the lawn toward her roofless hut. She motioned for me to follow.

"Why don't you explain it to me? We have about ten minutes before Nemain gets here with her guards, and then it'll be too late."

"Her guards and Balor." Caer's dark hollow eyes flashed. "Finally, you two will pit your power against each other once again."

My heart squeezed tight. "You can't want that. With everything you know and everything you've shown me, I don't understand why you would want such a thing."

She picked up a mug from her tiny little wooden table and handed it to me. It was still hot, steaming. She'd only brewed it moments ago, clearly foreseeing my arrival, clearly foreseeing that we would have this chat. And then she passed me a pair of dark trousers, along with a flowing tunic a vicious shade of red.

"My Morrigan, do you know what I am?" she asked, surprising me.

Frowning, I took a sip of my mug. "You are Caer, the Goddess of Prophecies and Dreams, and—"

"I am not a goddess. That was simply a term one of you fae came up with to explain me. I am a druid, Morrigan. And I come from your lands. Once, there were hundreds of us. But when your power destroyed our realm, we had to flee. There are others like me out there, but I do not know of them. I am lonely here. I wish to return to my home."

Druid. Yes, that was what they'd once called themselves. Back in Faerie, they had lived harmoniously by our side. Their magic was different than ours. Purer, in a way. They sought the earth for comfort, delving into prophecies of the future and signs from the past.

I hadn't made the connection to who they'd once been, not until now.

"I'm sorry," I said. "I wish I could go back and undo what we did. I wish I could make Faerie a home once again. But—"

"Hear me now, Clark Cavanaugh." Her voice suddenly went deep, so deep that fear skittered along my skin. "*You can.*"

Thunder clapped overhead, causing me to jump halfway out of my skin. I opened my mouth to ask Caer what she meant, but she was gone. She vanished into her hut, stealing the mug from my hands.

*Nemain is here…*a soft voice whispered on the wind.

But where the hell was Kyle?

Sucking a deep breath into my lungs to steady myself, I turned toward the distant hillside where I knew Nemain would appear. I was still trying to make sense of Caer's words. What did she mean, I could go back and undo the damage we'd caused? If only that were true, I would do anything to make it right.

But I couldn't focus on that now. Not when Nemain and an army of her warriors appeared at the edge of the tree line. She stood out in front, her entire body clad in leather armour. Two dozen Fianna fanned out on each side.

My heart went silent for far too long when I spotted the male who stood beside her.

It was Balor.

He stood beside Nemain.

His sword was in his hands.

And it was pointed at me.

Tears flooded my eyes as a pain so great and deep ripped through the very core of me. Even as angry as

I'd been, there'd been a part of me that hadn't fully believed Balor would ever turn on me. A part that had hoped with bated breath that his betrayal had been nothing more than a lie.

But there he stood, his muscular form backlit by the brilliant sunset.

I swallowed hard and suddenly felt very alone.

"Where is Caer?" Nemain called out. "Where is the crown?"

I cleared my throat, closed my eyes, and called upon every ounce of courage I had. No matter how much this hurt, there was no turning back now. I had to carry on with the plan and ignore the shockwaves of pain churning through my body.

All I had to do was get through this.

Then, I could concentrate on Balor.

"She's not here," I called up to Nemain.

My enemy shifted on her feet, clearly annoyed by my answer. "Stop playing games, Clark."

"I could say the same damn thing to you."

She scowled, and her voice dropped lower. "Listen, you mongrel. You better tell me where the hell my crown is, or I will make sure that your precious friends are destroyed."

Aed and Midir, the purple-haired fae, appeared from the forest with Tiarnan and Ronan chained between them. My heart leapt into my throat when I saw my friends. Hope and fear roiling through me all at once. They were alive.

That was all I needed to see.

They were alive.

But then Nemain twisted a knife into my gut.

"Give me the crown and end this ridiculous charade of you as Queen. Or I will kill them both."

My heart lurched at her words, even though I had expected them. Nemain knew where to kick me. She knew what made me tick. Threatening my friends was an express ticket to cooperative Clark.

"Okay, okay." I held up my hands, letting her see that I was giving in. "I'll do whatever you want. Just don't hurt my friends."

"That's what I thought." Her teeth flashed as she smiled. "Now, come here, and hand over the crown."

"I can't. It's not here."

A long moment passed in silence. "Explain."

"I can't really explain," I said. "But I can show you."

She hesitated for a moment, but then she strode down the rolling hillside. My heartbeat was frantic; my mouth dry. This was what we had wanted. All we had to do was get her into Faerie, and Jake would do the rest. When she reached me, I pointed at the Lake.

"We're going in there," I said.

She narrowed her eyes. "You first."

I shrugged and jumped in. Once again, I swam through the sparkling waters of the portal, leading Nemain from the mortal realm and into the ancient lands of the fae. I didn't look behind me to see if she had followed. I knew she had. She wouldn't be able to stop herself, her desire for power too great, her curiosity insatiable.

When I reached the other side, I pushed up out of the water and waited while Nemain joined me in the grass.

Nemain gaped as she glanced around. "It's been here this whole time?"

"I thought you knew."

She cast me a frown. "Of course I didn't know. If I had, I would have come back here to draw upon its power. Can't you feel it, humming in the air?"

Indeed I could, but I hadn't the last time I'd been here. The world had felt dead then. Decaying, full of ash.

But life hung in the air like a song, just waiting for an instrument to be played.

Fae after fae popped up from the lake, including Balor. There were about ten of them now, not including Nemain or me. This, I hadn't planned on. The more fae that joined us inside of Faerie, the harder it would be to isolate Nemain to trap her here. How would I draw the others back through the portal without bringing her along with them?

Another Fianna popped through, dragging a half-drowned form along with him. He hoisted the body from the lake and tossed him onto the ground before us. Jake sputtered up half a lung, his eyes bleary as he stared up at me. My stomach twisted into knots.

"Look what I found," the fae spat. "Lurking in the bushes, lying in wait."

32

It took everything within me to stand my ground. Somehow, Nemain's warriors had found our sorcerer, and they'd brought him here, ruining our entire plan. How had that even happened? And where the hell was Moira?

I fought the urge to pace back and forth, to dig my hands deep into my hair and scream. Jake was the only one who knew how to close the damn portal, and now he was stuck on the wrong side of the Lake of the Dragon Mouth with the rest of us.

If he wasn't ready and waiting to close the portal when I swam back over to the other side, there was no guaranteeing we would have enough time to cast the spell.

Which meant we had no chance of trapping Nemain…

I closed my eyes, breathing in the strangely fresh scent that peppered the air. Magic caressed my skin, igniting memories of my time here so many years ago. The ground beneath my feet pulsed in time with my heartbeat. This place still looked as dead as it had days ago, but the *feel* of it, the magic, was so different than it had been before. What had changed?

"A sorcerer." Nemain snorted. "You thought you could take me out with the help of a single sorcerer. I have to hand it to you, Clark, I didn't see that one coming."

Balor still hadn't said a word. He stood glowering in the pack of Fianna, his lips pressed tightly together. He had sworn fealty to Nemain, which I supposed meant he was bound to her the way the rest of the Court was. She must have ordered him to stay silent, knowing it would get under my skin.

Annoyingly, it was working.

"Now, where's the damn crown?" Nemain turned in a slow circle, eyeing up the abandoned bank of the lake. I had wondered how long it would take her to notice that neither Caer nor her precious crown were anywhere to be seen.

"I've got to be honest with you. I don't have a clue. Caer kind of does what Caer wants, and wherever she went, she took the crown."

Nemain's face transformed into a vicious shade of red. Her eyes went alight with fire; her fisted hands shook by her sides.

"You said you would take me to the crown," she said in a hiss.

"I lied." I shrugged. "I was really trying to lure you into Faerie. Did you anticipate me doing that?"

"Why?" She stalked toward me, waving her hands frantically. "What would be the point? You have no one here, just like you have no one back in your mortal realm either. They're all gone, or they're all mine. You have no one, Clark. Not even here."

A dark smile spread across her face. "You don't even have Balor Beimnech."

And there it was. The punch in my face. The stab in my heart. The knife, twisted in my gut. I could barely breathe from the force of the blow, from the pained magic skittering up my arms.

I ground my teeth, desperately trying to hold it back. But the wound was deep, her words so sharp. There was nothing I could do to stop my skin from leaking it all out. The pain tore out of me like a rage, filling up the sky with white hot power.

Nemain's eyes danced as she watched the magic spill from my soul. Something inside of me stirred. The mere whisper of something, something that felt as familiar to my own body as my bones.

It felt like Balor.

Balor, who had betrayed me.

"That's it," Nemain said, clapping her hands together. "You don't have him anymore because he's mine."

Another punch to the chest. Another rush of fiery magic through my veins.

"He left your side, knowing that you betrayed him for the crown."

For a moment, my magic faltered, the cloud of rage dissipating in an instant. "Wait a minute. What are you talking about? I never betrayed Balor for the crown."

Across the field, our eyes locked. Balor cocked his head, the blank expression he'd painted onto his face now replaced by something else. Hope, confusion, and the same kind of pain I felt deep within my gut.

"He betrayed you," Nemain insisted. "And you betrayed him."

I saw what she was playing at now. If she had only kept her mouth shut, she might have gotten away with it. She had pitted us against each other, feeding us lies. Nemain still wanted us to use our power against each other, even here in Faerie. She wanted me to lose control. She wanted to prove to the rest of the fae that I could never be trusted with power.

Something poked at my brain. Immediately, I dropped all the barriers I held around my mind.

Nemain told me that you had secretly taken the deal with her. She showed me evidence, evidence that proved it to be true...

I frowned and hoped Nemain took the change in my expression as a response to her words, not the ones echoing inside of my mind.

What kind of evidence?

Video surveillance footage of you taking the crown. Footage that was later deleted when Kyle went missing. She told me that you'd killed him...but that cannot be true, can it?

I narrowed my eyes, and for a moment, I was too angry to respond. Of course there'd been security footage of me taking the crown. And of course Nemain would use that against me however she could.

But if she already knew about the crown, then why had she come here? My heart thumped hard. She'd been expecting something like this. Some kind of lure to get her out of the Court. And yet...she'd let it happen.

What is she playing at? I asked Balor through our mental bond.

ALL'S FAE IN LOVE AND WAR

She wants us to fight. She wanted to get us in the same damn place so that we could finally clash our powers together. She's been trying to turn us against each other.

I flicked my eyes toward Nemain, pulse racing. She was clever, I'd give her that, but not clever enough. Regardless of whether she anticipated this trap, she hadn't known we would come into Faerie. She came willingly, which also suggested she did not realise that magic could not translate between the two realms. Everyone on the other side of the portal was no longer bound to her, at least not until she returned.

Of course, that meant that everyone here still was.

Maybe we could use this to our advantage. Maybe we didn't need Jake to trap her here. Maybe there was some other way we could end this here and now, and never take the fight back into the mortal realm.

What are you thinking? Balor's voice echoed in my mind.

Our gazes locked. Everything within me called out to him. Seeing him now, I didn't know how I'd believed that he could ever betray me. He was not Baleros, the original Smiter who had burned this world to the ground. And I was not the Morrigan, who had betrayed my lover on the battlefield. We were reincarnations of their souls, but we were in possession of our own hearts and our own minds.

Our combined power scared the shit out of me. But we would never overcome it if we did not face it head on.

If she wants us to fight, then let's show her a fight.

I could feel the confusion rippling through Balor's thoughts in waves.

In the end, it won't be a real fight. The Morrigan and the

Smiter destroyed this world because their hatred was too great, too powerful. I don't hate you, Balor. I could never hate you, not even if you truly had betrayed me.

Balor didn't answer. Instead, he stepped forward out of the rows of Fianna and stood in the middle of the field alone. Nemain's eyes went wide, and delight flickered through her churning irises. With a deep breath, I strode forward to meet him.

The world dropped away as I looked up into his orange eye.

"Hello, Morrigan," he said, the words out loud this time.

"Smiter," I said. "It has been a long time."

"Are you ready for this?" he asked. One last chance to walk away from this. But we couldn't. Running in fear of our bond had been my choice. And it had been wrong. It had only put off what we knew we had to face. Each other. I'd pushed it aside, tried to tamp it down, but the only way to overcome our past was to accept it, warts and all.

Caer had tried to tell me, time and time again, but I never listened.

I let out a long, slow exhale and then readied myself for whatever would come next. "It is now or never, Balor Beimnech. Why don't you finally show the world your orange eye?"

He flipped up his patch, keeping his eye squeezed tight. His entire body trembled from the force of it. His hands were curled into fists, and the silver-streaked hair became a storm of dancing strands.

At the sight of him open and bare to the world like this, my love for him overpowered everything else in my heart. My own hands became fists, but not in rage.

That white hot power curled around me, and I aimed my Morrigan magic right at the center of Balor's chest.

Whether he heard or felt my magic hurtling toward him, he knew it was coming.

He opened his eye.

The power clashed into each other. A boom shook the earth. It knocked me off my feet, skittering me meters away from where I'd just stood. I fell hard, my teeth slamming together. For a moment, my ears rang and I found it hard to see. The whole world was blurry before me.

Had we just done what we'd done before? When my vision cleared, would I be seeing nothing but flames?

"Oh my god!" I heard Jake's squeal and the clap of his hands before I saw him.

Before I saw *it*.

The world blurred back in before me, and for a moment, I thought our collide of magic had somehow transported us back into the mortal realm. The ground beneath my feet was green, and the clouds in the sky had cleared, revealing an ice blue that blinded my eyes. But then I saw the remnants of ash sprinkled throughout the ground. The dead trees in the distance. The tiny blooms coming to life.

My heart pounded hard in my chest. We were still in Faerie, but it was not the dead world we'd known only moments before. This one was full of life.

New life.

"I knew you would do it." Caer, leaning on an old wooden staff, scuttled out from the shadows of the nearby trees. She gave me a smile, and then turned her back on us all. "You brought my world back to life."

I had no idea how we'd done it. Something about the magic reversing itself perhaps. All I knew was that Balor and I had defeated whatever darkness had been brewing between us. Instead of death and decay, our combined magic had brought life.

I turned to face him with a smile. Instead, I found Nemain.

33

My eyes drank in my enemy. Ashes had fallen around her. No one else had been hurt when our magic combined, but Nemain's hand had been burned to a crisp. All that was left was a blackened husk.

Her eyes widened as I stalked toward her. She took a step back, her charred hand dropping her own sword. "You cannot fight me like this. I am unarmed."

I tightened my grip on my sword and held my ground. "I can't let you go."

"Well, you're going to have to fight us first." Aed and the rest of the Fianna surrounded us, quickly putting space between me and Nemain. They all held their swords, weapons ready and waiting.

A smile crested Nemain's lips. "You may have somehow bested your terrible power, but the bond with the Court still remains mine. The Fianna fight for me. And we greatly outnumber your army."

It was true. There were far more of them than us. But I had Balor, and his flaming orange eye.

"Clark," Balor said, his voice a warning. When I turned to face him, he gestured toward his eye.

But I didn't understand what he meant.

What's wrong?

His sigh was a caress against my soul. *What we just did drained us of our magic. It will come back in time, but we're not ready to fight. You won't even be able to call upon your ravens. Faerie is drinking our power. It's the only way for it to come back to life. And there's no stopping it now, even if we wanted to.*

Shit. So, not only could I not use my whole shouting trick thing, I probably couldn't shift either. Balor didn't have his eye, which meant we couldn't take down our enemies in one single swoop.

It was us against them. And Nemain had our sorcerer.

Midir and Aed grinned from the front of their pack. They lifted their swords to rush at us, their smiles eager, their armoured boots at the ready. But before they came our way, the sound of a distant splash cut through the field.

We all turned to see Ronan and Tiarnan leading a pack of...I blinked, certain that I was somehow imagining things. Matteo, in his crisp white suit, strode beside four other members of the Circle of the Night. The vampires had somehow come to our aide.

Nemain screeched. "Stop where you are right this instant."

"Sorry, love," Ronan said in a low growl, sending a wink my way. "We aren't bound to you, so you can't order us around. Neither are the vamps."

"Or me," Tiarnan added. "Being a solitary fae sucks, but it does have its perks."

"How are you here?" I blinked at them. "Why are you here?"

We'd left them back on the bank of Caer's lake. They'd been guarded by Fianna.

"As soon as you two disappeared through that lake, some of the warriors decided they didn't want to follow her any damn more. So, they left. The others, we managed to take out." Ronan shrugged. "Kyle suddenly appeared with some kind of satellite phone, and we thought...who should we call for backup? Turns out it was the vampires, if you can believe it."

No, I could not believe it. Matteo had made it crystal clear that he had no intention of ever standing by the fae's side during any type of war. He wanted to save his own ass, and the asses of his people, far more than he wanted to save mine.

"Matteo?" I couldn't help but ask, staring at the vampire.

"The Mayor explained the lengths you went to in order to extract him from the Pack's home base." He lifted a single shoulder in a shrug. "I suppose the alliance is back on."

Brows arched, I turned back toward Nemain, who was standing in her fort of Fianna. Fianna who only followed her because of the bond. "Perhaps it is time for you to admit defeat. You lost, Nemain."

She blinked at me for a moment, and then let out a snort of a laugh. "I have done nothing of the sort."

"You're here, alone, with no one to support you but a handful of Fianna." I gestured behind me. "There are more of us, and you no longer have the support of the fae."

She waved her hand dismissively. "Some trick of

the magic. I should have seen it coming. The bond doesn't work across realms, does it? That's why you wanted me to come here. But as soon as I return to the mortal realm, they will once again be under my command. Besides, vampires are not as strong as fae."

She lifted her hand and gave the signal.

The Fianna charged toward us on the freshly-blooming field. Gritting my teeth, I lifted my sword and held my ground. There were so many of them. Too many. We might outnumber them, but Nemain had been right. They were far stronger than we were right now.

"Sorcerer," Nemain crowed. "Cast your spell on these fae!"

"No, thanks." Jake jumped up when the Fianna released him, and he quickly joined in the fray, fighting alongside his vampire brethren.

Steel clashed against steel. A Fianna rushed at me, her sword swung wide at my head. I jumped to the side and ducked. It caught her off balance, and her body tipped to the side. Closing my eyes, I swung, and my blade sunk deep into flesh.

I ripped my blade from her fallen body and turned toward my next attacker. His weapon was a mace, sharp spikes sticking out of the wood. I ducked when he slammed it down from above. His approach was brute strength, not skill.

"Morrigan," Nemain called out from behind me. The Fianna I'd been fighting came to a sudden stop, his eyes glazed over. And then he drifted away, turning his attention to Tiarnan.

Letting out a low growl, I turned to face my ancient enemy. She stood alone on the hillside, the wind whipping her long dark hair. Her eyes were alight with fire, anger, and pure, unadulterated greed.

"As much as I would love to watch you fall on the blade of one of my warriors, you are mine."

I squared my shoulders and stalked toward her. "They are not your warriors."

She let out a light laugh. "You still believe they are yours, after everything that has happened? Even as they launch their weapons at your heart. You are the most delusional Morrigan I have ever met."

"Prove it then. Remove your control over them." I tightened my grip on my sword. "Tell them to no longer follow your commands, to do what they choose instead."

She ground her teeth together, her eyes flashing with rage. "Never."

"Then, I don't believe I am the delusional one here, Nemain."

She let out a scream of murderous rage and launched toward me. Her arms were outstretched, a dagger clutched tight in her one good hand. The blade made contact. It sliced through my thigh, slamming hard into the same place where I'd been wounded by Aed. Pain exploded through my leg, and I was on the ground instantly.

I clutched the wound, pressing my hands against the blood.

Nemain cackled and dove at me once again. I grabbed my sword from the ground and knocked her attempted blow to the side. She widened her eyes as she stumbled back, clearly not expecting my strength.

"Okay," she said, spinning the blade in her hand as she stalked in a circle around me. "Not bad. Still putting up a fight even though I got you pretty damn good in your leg. But just give up, Clark. You're not going to win. Not against me. Not without your powers. Even though I'm down a hand, I'm always going to be better than you."

My heart pulsed. I was afraid she was right. Nemain had trained for centuries. Sure, I'd been a fighter in my past lives but not in this one. My body wasn't used to it yet.

"You're just a half-fae. A mongrel. No one expects you to win a battle like this."

Anger roiled through my body. Gritting my teeth, I stood on my shaky leg, readying my sword before me. I was sick and tired of it. So done with people underestimating me because of where I'd been born. If she thought my shifter side would be a weakness, she had another think coming.

"Want to bet?" I asked.

She growled and rushed at me once again. This time, I was ready for her. I'd seen her do it twice before and knew how she moved. I easily blocked her blow, twisted around behind her, and wrapped my hand around her neck. I placed my blade against her throat and smiled.

"What were you saying about the mongrel?" I asked.

"Clark," she said, her body going still. No longer a mongrel, then. Not even a Morrigan now. "Please. You wouldn't kill me like this. That's not the kind of fae you are. You don't want to be a murderer like me."

I closed my eyes, still keeping a tight grip on her neck. I hated that she was right. It killed me that she knew how hard it was for me to end this fight the way

I knew I should. But we had come here to trap Nemain. If I didn't have to stab her in the heart, I wouldn't.

"Jake," I called out to where he was finishing off a Fianna with his fangs. "It's time to go back home."

He nodded, and I let go of Nemain.

This was the right thing to do. She could live out the rest of her days in Faerie. Hell, it wasn't a bad deal, not anymore. The world was coming back to life again and—

Nemain grabbed the sword from my hands and swung it at my head, one-handed.

The world seemed to slow around me. With eyes wide, I watched the blade arc toward me, watched the sharp edge slice right at my neck.

With a gasp, I ducked.

And then the world rushed in around me once again. Without even thinking, I kicked Nemain square in the stomach. She fell back, the blade falling from her hand as she hit the ground.

I caught the sword and took a breath.

The blade slid through her armoured chest, hitting her square in the heart. Magic rippled around me as her eyes slid shut. Blood spread across the growing grass, drenching the blades in red. A deep sigh echoed through Faerie, a shudder of something long held inside.

We were finally free.

EPILOGUE

There was much to take care of after Nemain died, her bond now fully broken for them all. For one, the wounded needed to be tended to, and the dead needed burying. I took that task upon myself. Beneath a tree now blooming with green, I dug grave after grave after grave. Even when the rain poured down from the sky, I didn't stop.

Their deaths were a tragedy, and I would not leave their bodies out on a bloody field to rot.

After every soul had been buried deep within the earth, I let Balor carry me away from it all. He took me back through the portal, put me in the car, wrapped a blanket over my shoulders, and drove me back to Court.

And then I got to work.

~

The fae of London stood at attention as I strode through the grand double doors that led into the throne room. Among them were scattered fae from around the world. Prior Princes and Princesses, Masters of Houses, and those few fae who had voted on the council of Faerie.

They all bowed as I walked between them, down a long, red carpet streaked with gold. With a deep breath, I kept my shoulders squared, thrown back, head held high.

The gown I wore was unlike any I'd ever seen before. Credne, the magical crafter, had spent the past few weeks diligently sowing a masterpiece. It was a dark crimson red, the sleeves cut short around my shoulders and the neckline diving low between my breasts. It was adorned with gold along the edges, tiny little flowers that spiralled around each other like dancing petals. The bottom drifted along the floor as I walked toward the dais, rustling with each move I made.

The voices of the Morrigans stirred within my mind as I took slow and steady steps toward the throne. I set my eyes on it and smiled. No longer did it converge on a pile of painted skulls, but wood-carved wings that flared out in a dramatic fashion behind it.

It had been Balor's idea, of course. I never would have suggested burning his throne. But he wanted it gone. He wanted to destroy the symbol of all the strife we'd both endured. Nemain had tried her damnedest to hold that throne between us, hoping we would take the bait and destroy each other in the process.

She had underestimated our bond. In the end, that had been her undoing.

Moira stood on the bottom step of the dais, clad in traditional warrior garb. Golden armour, a new sheath for her ever-present sword, and a ceremonial shield held by her side, carved with twin wings. Beside her sat an urn, decorated in silver, a memorial to Elise, who deserved to be here as much as those who had survived.

Kyle was near the front of the crowd, as was Ondine. They both smiled when I stepped past them, bowing their heads as I climbed. Even Henry was here, the sole human in the middle of a sea of fae. I'd met him just before the ceremony had started, and I'd told him the news. As part of my new rule, I was going to restart my podcast, keeping the humans and the supes of the city updated on the current developments of our world.

He'd been thrilled, his little arms twitching with anticipation. And I'd waited until the end to tell him the best of it: I wanted him to host it with me.

Tiarnan and Ronan stood just beside Henry. They'd both healed well from the battle, and Ronan had decided to stick around London instead of joining the Pack at the fort. Tiarnan, I planned to promote to the new Master of House Futrail, as soon as he'd had his induction ceremony. It was a distinction he deserved, and I knew he would serve them well.

The only missing contingency was the vampires. But Matteo was busy making deals with the Mayor, who had come through just as we'd hoped. As a new member of supernatural society, his grudge against us had vanished into the night. Peace had flooded the streets.

Even Aed was there, his purple-haired friend by his side.

Balor stood beside the throne, waiting for my approach. When I reached him, he stepped to the right and knelt. The crown he held was new. Wooden, carved with wings, to match the throne. The work of Credne, who had finally been given his position at the new Faerie Court: weapons master.

A hush fell over the crowd when the ancient violins silenced their song. Everyone bowed low and waited.

Balor cleared his throat and gazed up at me with an adoring eye, his burning flames still masked, though no longer a threat churning between us. We had sworn ourselves to love, to each other. There was nothing that could change that now.

"You are the Morrigan," he began, his voice ringing clear and loud in the expansive space. "The fae of this world wish to crown you their Queen. Will you accept this crown and all that it means?"

I gave a nod, tears staining my cheeks. "I will."

"Then, as the chosen spokesman of this Court, I now crown you Queen. Queen of all of Faerie."

∽

The fae celebrated as the fae always did. A ball. One full of singing, dancing, and drinking. I joined in, spinning from one grinning male to the next. Hours went by. Happiness had never felt so sweet. But my feet began to ache, and my arms got tired, and I found myself being spun out of the room by my very own mate.

He lifted me into his arms and carried me away from the party. I squealed, but I did nothing to stop him. I might be the Queen of Faerie, but I still liked being swept off my feet every now and again. Especially by a male like Balor. His magic caressed my skin as he took me up the stairs, kicking open the door of our penthouse.

It was ours now. Not mine and not his.

Ours.

He carried me to the bed and lowered me gently onto the pillows. I stared up at him, lovingly, wanting nothing more than to spend the rest of the night wrapped up in his arms. I might now be Queen, but that wasn't the greatest part of my night. It was Balor Beimnech, the male who had brought me to life when I hadn't even known how close I was to dead when he'd found me hiding away in that tiny flat.

"This is it, you know," Balor whispered into my ear. "We should make it count."

I pulled back and stared up into his gleaming eye. "What do you mean?"

"Caer said that we were it. The last of them. The final Smiter and Morrigan to ever live." He traced his finger along my jawline. "We are it."

I breathed him in deeply, wishing this moment could never end. We had endured so many lives together, forever entwined. It was impossible to remember a time that he was not in my life, because so many of my moments were with him.

"It doesn't feel like it's ending to me, Balor," I

couldn't help but say. "To me, it feels like it's just the start."

"Because we've finally defeated it," he said.

"Defeated what?"

"Whatever we did that day, centuries ago in Faerie, it started a chain of events that the magic couldn't stop," he said. "We had to end it ourselves. Our vows to each other, our love, it has stopped the reincarnations. Caer must have known all along. We were never going to end the world, but we had to think that we might. So that we were forced to prove we'd found love instead of war."

It made sense. Every single bit of it.

We had reversed the damage we did to Faerie, though we could never claim back all those lives that had been lost. The world bloomed once again, and hope now drifted across those brilliant green hills. In the end, we had decided to keep the portal open between the realms. Caer no longer stood watch at the Lake of the Dragon Mouth, but we would find a replacement, someone else to ensure the portal was never crossed by anyone unworthy.

One day, the fae would fill the streets of Faerie once again. Just not now. Not yet. Our home was here.

"So, what now?" I whispered.

He smiled. "You rule Faerie, and I stand by your side."

"You know what else?" I grinned.

"What is that, my love?"

"The fae have twined together to form one singular Court. The Crimson Court is no more, and you are no longer a Prince. That means your prophecy has no chance of ever coming true. Your son will not destroy you and the fae of London." I wrapped my arms around him and pulled him close. "There is nothing holding us back anymore."

∽

Thank you for reading The Paranormal PI Files! Next up, *Confessions of a Dangerous Fae*, now available for preorder on Amazon, will follow Moira as she spies on the fae of Edinburgh. Coming November 2019!

Sign up to my reader newsletter to be notified on release day.

AUTHOR'S NOTE

Thank you so much for reading this series. I've loved every minute of writing it, and I'm going to miss spending so much time with these characters and these settings.

Many of the locations highlighted in these books were inspired by real-life places in London and the surrounding areas.

For the new home of the Pack, I had a lot of fun reimagining the Red Sands Tower that stands abandoned in the Thames Estuary. Just as in this story, the forts are heavily rusted and sit on massive stilts above the water, and they haven't been used in years. In 2005, an artist called Stephen Turner lived in the Shivering Sands Tower, alone in isolation, for thirty-six days, and then wrote a book about the experience. It's called *Seafort*, if you'd like to check it out.

I've posted some photos of the various locations in my Facebook reader group if you'd like to see the real thing.

The Pack's new fort, along with many of the other

AUTHOR'S NOTE

locations Clark has visited, will be making brief appearances in the next series set in this world of supernaturals. But mostly, we'll be taking a trip further north to Edinburgh, a city with rich history and beautiful architecture. Moira, a character who I have grown to love far more than I expected when I first started writing this series, is getting her own story. She's had a prophecy from Caer, after all. And she's about to come face to face with it in the form of a sexy fae named Lugh.

ABOUT THE AUTHOR

Jenna Wolfhart is a Buffy-wannabe who lives vicariously through the kick-ass heroines in urban fantasy. After completing a PhD in Librarianship, she became a full-time author and now spends her days typing the fantastical stories in her head. When she's not writing, she loves to stargaze, rewatch Game of Thrones, and drink copious amounts of coffee.

Born and raised in America, Jenna now lives in England with her husband, her two dogs, and her mischief of rats.

FIND ME ONLINE
Facebook Reader Group
Instagram
YouTube
Twitter

www.jennawolfhart.com
jenna@jennawolfhart.com